A
LAND
CALLED
BOUNTIFUL

KIRBY JONAS

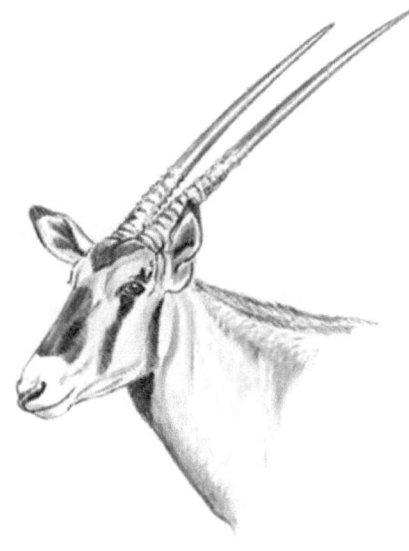

A
LAND
CALLED
BOUNTIFUL

Howling Wolf Publishing
Pocatello, Idaho

Howling Wolf Publishing
1611 City Creek Road
Pocatello ID 83204

For more information about Kirby's books, check out:

http://www.kirbyjonas.com
Facebook, at KirbyJonasauthor

Or email Kirby at: **kirby@kirbyjonas.com**

Manufactured in the United States of America—*One nation, under God*

First printing: 2015
Jonas, Kirby, 1965—
A Land Called Bountiful / by Kirby Jonas.

ISBN: 978-1-891423-17-8
Library of Congress Control Number: 2015957650

To Keith, my buddy, for all his hard work
And dedication, and his great big heart

"And it came to pass that we did pitch our tents by the seashore; and notwithstanding we had suffered many afflictions and much difficulty, yea, even so much that we cannot write them all, we were exceedingly rejoiced when we came to the seashore; and we called the place **Bountiful**, because of its much fruit."

—1 Nephi, 17:6, *Book of Mormon*

Chapter One

The Fury of Ari'el

The rocks and the dust were endless. The camels swayed like ships. Hour upon hour they plodded until some men would have wished death upon themselves.

The young man known as Nephi liked nature. He enjoyed the sight of the mountains, even barren as they might be, and the valleys, whether in winter or spring, when all was green and sprinkled with flowers, or in summer and fall, when the world lay crackly and dry under its coat of many browns. He loved the wispy, far up clouds, the thunderheads that boiled up like sheep's wool out of the horizon itself, or the glowering storm clouds that hung purplish black overhead, with rain bellies ready to burst. He loved sunsets and sunrises, rainbows, and soft, fluttery rain.

But the country around them had begun to seem monotonous now, the backs of the camels swaying, their riders rocking to and fro with their meaty humps. The mountain ranges seemed achingly alike unless one took the time to seek out their differences. And in this heat even Nephi, lover of nature, had no energy for that.

Under the shelter of his own shroud and his blue tunic and flowing robe, big Nephi watched the trail ahead, praying for swiftness, knowing that one more day would bring them to the camp of his father, Lehi, where all would rejoice. He could hardly blame them, but his older brothers, Laman and Lemuel and some of the others, perhaps worst of all his brother by marriage, Shedrar, had begun to complain bitterly of the heat. They talked of nothing more than a desire to return to Jerusalem, and even after witnessing Nephi's healing of the Bedouin people, their cynicism had quickly returned, and they appeared to have no faith whatsoever in the prophecies of Lehi. All of this made Nephi incredulous and sad. Could nothing change those who would murmur?

Nephi thought back on the Bedouin. Two days since, they had swarmed down upon them, shortly after a fierce battle of their own with some neighboring tribe. They had been bent on stealing the women with Nephi's group, and nothing was going to stop them. But then, through the power of Yahweh, Nephi had promised them that he would lay hands on their wounded people and heal them, some of them wounded nigh unto death in the recent battle. He would do this if they would set them free.

The miraculous healing which followed had made friends of the Bedouin, and Nephi had rejoiced, both for the friendship, and for the fact that he had believed hard-hearted Laman and Lemuel and the other dissenters among them would come to believe the truth, and come to believe in the power of Yahweh. Now Nephi could see it had not.

Sweat trickled into his eyes, and once again, wearily, he swept it away with the wide sleeve of his woolen robe. His dromedary, old patriarch Abraham, grunted wearily beneath him, turning his head to look at something—or at nothing. It was only the tired, drab, ragged mountains, the scraggly acacia trees that stood weary and forlorn, forever imprisoned in place by their own roots and the dull, endless, trackless sand.

For some time that morning he had had company, first his promised bride, Rachel, then his friends Lotan and Yona, then Yael, whom he had rescued from her brutal father, and even his younger sister, Tikvah, and for a long while brother Sam. But those had all dropped farther back into the line now, and even here, where the trail stretched out to ten or twenty miles wide, the caravan of camels tramped along in single file, because no one had the energy to speak to another. Unless it was to speak of no good...

Some time back, they had veered from the main frankincense trail that led down to the coast. Now they followed the track that Father Lehi had taken, hugging tight, where they could, to the Gulf of Aqabah, the fountain of the Red Sea.

Nephi heard camels coming up on him, and he sighed. He knew that talking might keep him awake, yet he was so tired, his lips cracked and mouth full of cotton. He desired only to keep his mouth shut, to ride on until the cool of evening, when he could rest. He wanted to be able to travel at night, in the way of all wise desert wanderers of the ages, yet he did not know this trail well enough, and to miss even one of the oases might be to die.

To his surprise, the first person he saw riding up beside him was Shedrar, and on the other side came Laman and Lemuel. There were no others. As there had been little talk during the breaking of camp that morning, he did not know where the thoughts of these three were going, other than of course the end-less complaining about the heat and wind.

To Nephi himself, the spirit in camp that morning had seemed one of reverence, after all that everyone had witnessed during the healings. He wished that were still the case. It was possible that these three had come to apologize for how they had been acting. If that were so, then Nephi would gladly speak with them. They had not seemed to be friends for a very long time.

"Nephi," said Shedrar, and Nephi looked at him and nodded. This man, his sister Tikvah's husband, looked at him through eyes as black as any he had ever seen. "We have been speaking of these men who came nearly to our camp. I am told, and I would like to know from you if this is true, that they came here to kill or to capture your friends Lotan and Yona."

Shedrar had smiled a little at him, but to Nephi that meant nothing. He instantly felt trouble coming, and he was a bit surprised. He had thought that for at least a few days there would be mostly peace, and even the complaints about the desert he could handle, because that, he understood.

The men Shedrar was speaking of were a group from the Red Sea port town of Ezion-Geber who had come seeking for revenge on his friend Lotan, who had been in a fight with the family of the woman he loved, Yona, and who had fled into the desert with her. It had been a strong contingent of men, and they would have surely attacked the camp of Nephi and the others, but the Bedouin people forced them to return the way they had come.

"I admit that is true, Shedrar."

"Then we find it interesting that you allowed Lotan and Yona to join us on our journey without begging leave of us, your elders who have charge of this company. You seemed to think nothing about the trouble they might bring."

"For that I apologize, but I could not leave them there alone, on foot in this desert."

"I can understand that," cut in Laman. "And they seem to be decent enough people, even if Yona seems a little haughty for my taste. But some kind of warning would have been in order, I think."

"Yes, what if we had been alone at that camp when they came?" asked Lemuel. "I know you well enough, little brother, to know that you would not have freely let them be taken, so you would have started a fight."

"You are right, Lemuel," Nephi admitted tiredly. "I would not have freely let them go."

Lemuel slapped his leg. "See? And then we would all have become involved, and it would have been our small party against their fifteen or more. And they were probably all well-armed, most likely better than we, and were not accompanied by women and children they would have to protect."

Nephi found himself wanting to urge Abraham into a long lope, to step away from these who would badger him—about nothing, as it turned out. He did not want to bandy words. He only wanted peace.

"Because I made friends with the Bedouin we were protected," he said, immediately regretting that he had singled himself out with his use of the word *I*. "We did for them a good turn, made them our friends, and they protected us. So all is well. And if you'll remember, Laman, it was you who wanted to fight the Bedouin, by far a larger force than ours—I asked everyone not to."

To admit that these things were true would be a weakness for these three men when all they wanted was to chastise Nephi for his impudence, so Shedrar jumped back in with, "That is not the point, Nephi. The point is that you, the youngest man in our group, who is hardly a man at all, took this danger upon our entire family without so much as a warning to us. We had no chance even to think on it or to plan for the eventualities. It is not your place, as a mere child, to take this responsibility on our group. Do you not understand?"

With resignation, Nephi said, "Yes, I understand," only to shut the others up.

"I would hope that you do," said Laman. "But I doubt the truth of it. You have been lording it over us since we first left Jerusalem with our father. And you tell us you will stop now?" Laman scoffed, and in anger, seeming to have wanted more of a fight than Nephi was giving back, he backed his camel off and rode back in line. Lemuel, now that his ringleader was gone, followed suit. But Shedrar stayed.

"I have another thing to say to you, Nephi. Your sorcerer's tricks do not convince me of anything, no matter if you have swayed your brothers for a while. You are no more a prophet of God and a worker of wonders than I am a red-eyed hippopotamus. I do not know how you did the things that you did for those Bedouin, but it was not of God. More likely it was of the devil.

"You stay away from my wife, Nephi. I don't need her head full of this rubbish, and I have listened to nothing from her this morning but how great her brother is and how he saved us all from certain doom. So with the help of the devil you are turning my wife against me. You stay away from Tikvah, boy, or I will see you dead and know well that it was a service to the true God of Israel."

With that threat, Shedrar followed Nephi's brothers back in line, and Nephi sat his camel with his teeth clenched. A bad spirit had gotten into Shedrar long ago, and now it was plain that nothing was going to make it go away. If that man could go through that night's miracles and not see the power of God he never would. Lucifer, the fallen son of God, was strong in Ishmael's second son.

Shortly after their talk, Nephi heard Joab asking for a halt. In the suspicion that had overcome him now he assumed it was only because Joab and the other three men were trying to assert their authority as the rightful leaders here. Nephi turned as Ishmael was agreeing, and they all circled their camels in, bedded them down and dismounted.

There was no shelter out here, so they took one of the woolen tents from the back of a camel and set it up, without the sides, to shade Ishmael and the women and children. It was large enough that the men could crowd under the shade, too, but Nephi chose not to, and before those who would not want to sit with him had realized his choice they had also seated themselves out in the sunshine.

Nephi sat with his back to the shelter, and Sam came and sat beside him, then Lotan and Yona. Soon, Rachel appeared, and the sight of her made Nephi's heart swell.

She came around him and sat down in front, nestled up against him. A lot of mores that would have been observed in polite society had been set free out here. In Jewish society, a future bride and groom who were betrothed were not even to associate with each other until their wedding. But soon, seeing her younger sister's example, Ari'el also came and sat in front of Sam. Ishmael and Ra'ya did not even seem to take note.

Nephi did not turn to see, but he heard movement behind him and knew that his older brothers and the sons of Ishmael had removed themselves under the shelter of the lean-to, now that they knew they did not have to share it with the likes of him. There was plenty of room now, and the air inside would not be tainted for them by Nephi's breath.

"I have been thinking about traveling up into the mountains, if ever we draw close, and killing an ibex or a goat," said Laman suddenly. "Perhaps I will break away and do that when we are a few miles from tonight's camp."

Laman had addressed no one in particular, so for a few moments there was silence. Then Nephi heard Ishmael say, "I think that would be fine, my son. If you find a large one, after we have eaten our fill we can salt and hang the remainder of the meat on the packs of the camels as we travel and dry it for harder times."

Looking down, Nephi smiled to himself. Harder times! Ishmael was a real man, he thought. They had already been through some very hard times—particularly Ishmael himself. He hoped they were through the hardest. Unfortunately, he had no way to be prepared for what they were heading into.

Their worst enemy yet bore the ominous name of Rub' al Khali...

Nephi listened to the quiet talk behind him in the tent. He wished he could feel a part of it, but after the harsh words of his brothers, and especially of Shedrar, he did *not* feel a part. In his heart he said a prayer, asking for inner strength. He did not have the heart at that moment to pray that Laman, Lemuel and Shedrar would be softened. Perhaps another time...

He had no more than finished praying when he heard Shedrar laugh and say, "So, Nephi, any more conjurer's tricks up your sleeves today? I for one would like to see more of your black magic."

"Hush, Shedrar," said Ra'ya. "Be still."

"Oh, Mother, he knows I am having fun with him."

Sam suddenly got up and whirled around facing the shelter. "You are not having fun with him! I have heard you and my elder brothers speak. You should be filled with shame, Shedrar. You blame Nephi for sorcery. You say he is not a man of the Lord but a pretender, a sorcerer and a conjurer of spells. But if Nephi had not agreed to let the power of the Lord work through him to heal those Bedouin, they were going to take six of our women. And who knows what else?"

There was only a moment of silence, for the devil was thinking for some of the people there that day, and the devil is fast to find new cracks in a wall.

"That is another thing!" Laman barked, standing up and coming out of the shelter. He ignored Sam, even though he was the one who had spoken, and concentrated his anger on Nephi, who was still seated. "What if you had not healed those people? They were going to kill two of our men, Nephi. They were going to burn one of our daughters in the fire and take not six but *all* of our women, and all of the children as slaves. And all because you had to open your mouth and offer to heal those people who brought their own wounding upon themselves."

Nephi stood up, but he was too stunned to speak. By the power of the Lord he had made friends with the Bedouin tribe and possibly saved every member of his family. Laman was blinding himself to the plain fact that Bahram had planned on taking six of their women away, no matter what else happened. One of them would have been Ra'ya, and one would have been Rachel. And it was in every way possible that Ze'eva, Laman's promised bride, would also have been in that number. But Laman was too full of hate and jealousy to see this, and Nephi too shocked to point it out. Ari'el, however, was not.

Sam's future bride stood up and whirled on Laman, her eyes full of righteous fire. All of the group who had chosen to remain outside the shelter got up with her and faced the others. Ari'el, for a terrible moment, glared her disdain at Laman, and then she spoke, and her voice was like the voice of a lion in its intensity.

"You cannot truly be such a fool. I am sorry if I am speaking out of turn, if I am not acting as the daughter of Israel you expect me to be. But believe me, I would say much more if I could. Instead, all I will say is that you are a pitiful fool, a jealous fool, a fool who does not even need his younger brothers to make him so.

"There were going to be six of us taken away to live in the harems of the Bedouin, perhaps one of them your promised bride. We had no choice. It was already decided. And you, with all your brave talk, did nothing.

"But let us be honest—there was nothing you *could* do, for the spirit of the Lord dwells not within you. Nephi could do something, however, and Nephi did. Because he listened to the voice of the Lord inside him we not only were spared more torture at the hands of those savages, but they became our friends and then also saved Lotan and Yona from those who had come for them.

"I am tired of sitting idly and listening to you grumble about Nephi and what he has done, when you, Laman, Lemuel and Shedrar, have done nothing. And you, Zipporah, you cry over your child and blame Nephi for his death when we all heard you refuse in your anger to let Nephi bless him. I am sorry that your child died. I do not know how you can deal with the grief. But it is not Nephi's fault, and if you must find fault then you must find it in yourself, no matter how it hurts."

By the time Ari'el was finished speaking, there were tears staining her cheeks, the tears of her indignation and fury. And she was not alone in those tears.

"Let us go from this bad place," growled Joab, standing up under the shelter and walking into the sun. "There is no point in wasting time. The camels have rested and so have we."

While Ishmael and Ra'ya looked at the people around them, then gazed sadly at each other, the men began gathering up the shelter to pack it, and within twenty minutes the caravan was on its way again. This time there were two distinct groups of travelers, far apart from each other, and Ishmael and Ra'ya rode together an equal distance between the two.

Ishmael swayed in his saddle, his eyes sad, his face gray.

Chapter Two

The Pride

They were still some five miles away from their next stop, the last stop before reaching Lehi's camp, when Laman spotted a Nubian ibex far up on the mountain. They had come very close to the foot of the mountain, for the trail here was only several hundred yards wide.

The ibex, its majestic, ribbed black horns glinting in the sunlight, all of two and a half feet long and curving way out over its back, gazed at them from its impenetrable mountain lair. It looked royal, and somehow haughty, with its long, shaggy beard dangling down beneath its jaw like that of a king.

"I will bring us supper," said Laman with a grin. "Is anyone else in the mood for a hunt?"

Of course it went without saying that Laman's shadow, Lemuel, turned his camel aside to accompany his brother. Nephi was surprised to see Shedrar also draw out of the group, surprised because he did not expect Shedrar to so soon leave Tikvah alone in the presence of her evil brother who in Shedrar's opinion was trying to draw her off into the influence of the devil. Shedrar had no bow, but like all of the men he carried a sling for throwing stones and might come across a grouse or a partridge.

The two brothers and their cohort lumbered away on their camels toward the foot of the mountains, and the rest of the caravan continued on. Laman and Lemuel knew where the next encampment lay, so there was no need to wait for them.

They rode along the foot of the mountains for a time, since the ibex Laman had seen disappeared shortly after they approached. It was only three hours away from sunset, and the day was cooling down, so Laman, Lemuel and Shedrar began to be in good spirits. They laughed and joked and relived their memories of Jerusalem.

Shedrar remembered a time when, as a seven-year-old, he had wet himself at the religious school Ishmael had sent them to during one summer after harvest, and he tried to blame it on another little boy who sat near him. In spite of his own embarrassment and the fear of being caught, it had been pretty hilarious until the adults discovered that the boy who had been blamed was in fact dry and started looking around for the real culprit.

Shedrar had fought tooth and nail not to go back to the school after that humiliation, but of course his parents had forced him to. His only comfort had been Joab convincing him that if he ever had to urinate so badly again he should stand and do it straight on the other boy and at least then perhaps they would expel him from the school permanently.

Laman and Lemuel told a story about pretending to hang Nephi from the rafters of their house when he was six, and how they had barely been able to get the knot loose and had been forced to offer him half of their supper to get him to keep quiet and to hide the burns on his neck. "Sometimes I think it would have been better to let him hang," lamented Lemuel.

"You'd better stop that!" Laman countered. "He might conjure up some evil spell for you."

They all laughed, but Shedrar quickly stopped. "I would like to conjure up some spell for him! Do you suppose the beasts would actually devour him if we left him tied up in the wilderness? Or would he taste as strong as he thinks he is?"

Laman and Lemuel laughed, but Laman was not sure he thought it was too funny. This was, after all, their brother Shedrar was talking about.

"Let us tie the camels here," Laman said suddenly, as they neared a place where the rocks had tumbled down out of the high mountains and made a massive garden of stone amid the sand. There was no argument from his companions, so they made the camels lie down and climbed off.

As Laman came around his camel, Naomi, Ari tried to nip him, simply out of playfulness, and Laman swatted at Ari's face. "You should teach your camel better manners," Laman chided his brother. "Now my camel, she is a gem."

As he spoke, Naomi raised her nose to him, he lowered his face to her, and they nuzzled each other. He put his hands on either side of her face and caressed her cheeks as he looked into her vast dark eyes, seeing the lashes reflected inside them, along with the mountain ridge.

"You are a good girl," Laman said softly, scrubbing her head with his fingernails. He dug a finger into one of her ears and scratched, and she leaned into his hand, closing her eyes in her ecstasy. A flea jumped away from her, and he caught it, but when he opened his hand it escaped to the sand.

Lemuel laughed. "Why do you think you need Ze'eva when you already have Naomi, brother? Will you take two wives? Or will you send Naomi away on the night of your wedding?"

"Ah, Lemuel, don't be foolish. If I have to choose between Ze'eva and Naomi, I will always choose Naomi. I have never been married, yet I have seen the afflictions a woman can bring to her man. A camel brings no such afflictions.

"My Naomi has never asked for new sandals, or a new robe. She has never begged me for purple dye, or a necklace, or a ring of emeralds and gold. She has never spent too long making her hair curled and her eyes pretty. In fact, how could you improve on this?"

He laughed, putting his hand under Naomi's chin and lifting her face up for Lemuel to judge. As if playing her part, Naomi turned her face to one side, posing, her large upper lip hanging out over the lower one, her nostrils flared.

"You are right, Laman!" said Shedrar with a laugh. "Now *there* is a face, and a woman to be desired. I must say, if Tikvah looked so good we would surely have one or two more children by now—I could not stay away from her!"

Laman winked at Shedrar and ruffled the curly hair on Naomi's forehead. "That's my girl. The most beautiful in all the land. Wait for us, girl, and we will return with a morsel for you." With that, he took his wooden bow and drew it back, pretending to sight along his arm to some invisible mark on the mountain. He eased the pressure off the bow and looked at his comrades. "Let us be off!"

They climbed up into the thick rocks, picking their way carefully. After a time, each man found himself alone, and Laman began thinking of Nephi and of the events of two nights before. He envisioned the harsh, fierce face of Bahram, the sheikh, and the drawn faces of his older wives. He recalled how ill the wounded people had looked in their litters under the trees.

What had happened there? Had he really felt what he remembered feeling? It had made tears come to his eyes—yea, even to fall down his cheeks. And it had done the same to Lemuel, and even to Shedrar. So why was it that none of them could admit this even two days later? None of them would confess those tears, not even to each other, and all had seen them. A strange and wonderful spirit had fallen over the camp, and there had been a power there that Laman had never felt.

Why could not that feeling of power have been brought there by Laman himself? It would have made his people proud, and they would have hailed him as a true leader. He would have been able to stand over them with authority, and they would have known that he was a man of the true God, and that he would lead them in righteous ways. Why did it have to be Nephi? *Nephi!*

Laman cursed. Why would the God of Israel come and speak directly to one who was but a mere boy? Why, when there were eleven men his elder, and now twelve, if Lotan counted among them? It made no sense. And more than that, it simply rankled Laman.

Nephi seemed so self-righteous about it all, so much like he had been chosen their leader. In fact, had he not come right out and made that claim? That the Lord had appointed him as a leader over them? What kind of God would do that? Society demanded that the oldest son of a family, barring some infirmity that prevented it, be the natural leader, the one who made any decision in the absence of the father. No God would go against the established rules of an entire society. No *true* God.

The angel that had appeared to them in the cavity of the rock had spoken it too, he remembered–that Nephi had been chosen to be their leader. But now he did not know if that angel had really appeared, or if it had only been a trick of the mind.

They all joked about it, and Shedrar was especially bold about speaking it, but what if Nephi truly was a sorcerer? What if he was a conjurer, a wizard, dealing in black magic, working through the power of the devil? Who was to know? The devil had power too—not just the Lord. Who was to say that he could not heal those Bedouin people, if it suited his own purposes?

Either way, it did not set well with Laman to have a man who was no more than an overgrown boy lord it over him when all in the family knew who the rightful heir to Lehi's authority was.

He had a sudden memory of coming home from a journey to Egypt with Ishmael, and of Nephi, then four years old, coming to him on the run with a huge smile of love and joy on his face. Nephi could not reach him fast enough. He had seemed ready to climb straight up the side of his camel if that was what it took, to get to his big brother and throw his arms around him.

Laman had felt like a king to have this little boy love him so. All the rest of that day, although he had been exhausted from the trip, he had doted on his little brother. He had let him play with his new bow and his arrows, weapons he had purchased in Egypt. He had even let him sip of some special wine of a kind one could only find in Egypt.

Now, all these years later, Nephi was trying to take all of his authority away and make himself look like a big man. What had happened to that little boy, the one with so much respect and love? Laman grimaced. Sometimes he hated his little brother. And sometimes he loved him more than he would ever tell a soul, and was proud enough of him to burst.

Even amid all his soul-searching, Laman was still a hunter, and he finally found another herd of ibex. The Nubian ibex, like all goats, could perform unbelievable acrobatics, and they haunted the steepest, most forsaken cliffs imaginable.

Sometimes they would study a cliffside for what seemed mere moments, picking out a likely escape route, and then, in a mad dash, they would leap to the first outcropping, which might be no more than a one or two-inch shelf jutting out from the rock face, and then, in less than a second, leap to the next and the next and the next, until standing on some unreachable precipice a hundred yards away before an unready hunter could even begin to draw back his bow.

There was no animal in the world more agile and deft at the art of cliff scaling than the ibex, and they were every bit as skilled and as fast at coming back down those cliffs. Even the young, from a week or two old, were bouncing around through the rock faces as if there were no gravity.

Worse than their agility, as far as a hopeful hunter was concerned, the ibex always kept one or two sentinels watching for danger, and their senses of hearing, smell and sight were keen. But in Laman's favor was the fact that these ibex had probably never laid eyes on a human being, and it was literally their curiosity that did them in.

Laman stalked and killed an ibex—not the one of the great, massive horns that he had seen at first, but a young, tender nanny that weighed no more than a hundred and five pounds. The rest of the herd stood like so many bushes on the face of the cliff and watched him as he reached his prey and bent down to it with his knife.

He shouldered it after removing the head and innards and started down the mountain.

He had nearly reached the place where they had left the camels when he heard a horrible sound, the cry of a camel in distress. Startled, he stared over the rocks, trying to catch a glimpse of Naomi and the other beasts. He could not see them, but of a sudden he heard the sound that made a desert wanderer's blood freeze: the snarl of a lion!

Without thinking, Laman let the ibex drop off his shoulders and took off running through the rocks. He slipped once and fell, slamming his tail bone against a boulder, but he recovered and ran on, oblivious to the pain. He stopped a ways farther, checking only to make sure that his bow was not harmed and that all of his arrows were still there.

Then he continued running, his heart in his throat. The lion's roar came again, and then a second one, this one from a different lion. A camel cried again, and he was afraid he recognized the terror-filled voice.

As he came around the last huge boulder in his path, he ran almost directly into a pride of lions. There were six of them, one male, three females, and two half-grown cubs. They surrounded his Naomi, his horribly wounded Naomi, who lay on the ground with her legs folded under her, all but the right rear, which was stretched out and which the male lion was hovering over and tearing into with his horrible four-inch fangs.

Frozen in place, Laman stared in fear, his eyes misted with tears made by that fear. He began to back up, one slow step at a time. One of the lionesses and a cub had spotted him, and they stared at him intently, trying to understand what they were looking at. The lioness turned from Naomi and took a couple of tentative steps toward the new threat that might try to usurp their meal. The cub followed its mother, and Laman took another two steps back.

He raised his bow and drew an arrow from the quiver, nocking it almost without thinking. He pulled the string partway back as he kept inching backward. When at last he had disappeared around the boulder, he scrambled to pick up a handful of stones, one of them fairly large, and these he took with him and clambered up onto the boulder. It was only ten or twelve feet high, and he did not know if this was tall enough that a lion could not jump up on it, but he would not leave Naomi down there alone, not while she still had a chance.

With his bruised tailbone now aching, Laman crawled to the outer edge of the boulder. He heard a low growl and a weak mewling sound and turned to see the lioness and the cub rearing up with their front paws on the rock he now crouched atop. He was surrounded.

Laman looked long and hard at the lioness and cub that gazed up at him as if he were prey, but he knew he could waste no stone or arrow on them, not while Naomi was still alive.

He turned back to the male lion, and with all of his strength he unleashed a stone. Throwing rocks had been a pastime of Lehi's children for many years, since early childhood, and at this skill they were adept. The stone struck the lion just above the ear, and snarling, he slashed at his head with his massive paw and whirled around, trying to see what fool had dared harm him.

The closest being was the other cub, which crouched watching him ten feet away, trying to learn how to hunt and to kill a large prey animal. Furious at his pain and only able to blame it on one thing, the lion rushed the cub, but it darted away in terror and confusion. The lion chased it only a ways before turning back to the camel it had claimed. Another lioness had now pounced on the camel's hump, holding it down, and Laman slammed a rock into the bridge of its nose with all his might.

The lioness ducked and snarled in pain, then went running out across the sand before whirling around to see if it could catch the culprit. The lion watched her for a moment, his eyes obviously full of confusion. But having no idea what had happened or apparently no desire to try and figure it out, the lion moved in again for the kill, and Naomi moaned from deep in her throat, a pitiful, dejected, mournful sound that tore open Laman's heart.

Standing up to get more leverage, Laman screamed out at the top of his voice, and when the long-maned lion looked, it was struck between the eyes with a two-pound rock. The beast fell back on its haunches, roared and ran off to the other side of Naomi, then circled back around, its tail twitching. Laman had never seen fiercer eyes than these that stared him down. He knew instantly that the lion was going to make a try for him, to pull him off his rock. And he suddenly had no doubt the beast could do it.

However, before he could react, he heard scratching on the rock behind him and turned just in time to see the lioness crawling up onto the boulder with him. With all his might he hurled his fourth stone. It struck her in the teeth and made her fall backwards. Her reflexes and the height from which she fell only just saved her from landing on her back. Spinning, she landed on her feet and snarled, and Laman saw blood smeared on the front of her mouth and chin. The lioness and cub had had enough, and they loped off around the boulder and back to their pride mates.

But the male lion's assault had just begun.

Chapter Three

Beloved Naomi

With a snarl that made Naomi and Laman both cringe, the lion made a rush for the boulder, and he leaped.

Terrified, Laman had no time to react. The feet of the big cat reached the top of the boulder, and he started to gain a purchase with his steel-like claws. Instinctively, Laman kicked out and caught the big cat in the teeth, and it fell back with another snarl and landed sideways on the ground, but still on its feet. Circling away, and stopping near Naomi, it made ready for another rush.

Before Laman could even think, the lion ran for the rock, and this time he had his distance calculated from the first attempt. Fear filled Laman's entire being as he saw the lion obtain a purchase on the rock with his front claws. His back claws were digging in for a purchase, and now he had it! Desperately, Laman kicked out again, and the lion slashed out with both paws and caught his foot. A horrible, searing pain ran up through Laman's leg, and instinctively he swung with his bow, striking the lion alongside one eye.

The lion snarled and snapped at the end of the bow, catching it in his teeth. Laman knew he was dead. There was no god in heaven or on earth that could save him now, but like a cornered beast he fought savagely back, his last act of defiance.

With all his might, he bent far forward and swung a fist at the lion's soft, wet nose, and in pain and surprise the huge animal let go of his bow and his foot and reared back. Unfortunately for him, he went back just too far...

Like a landslide, the lion slid down the front of the boulder, at last letting go with his scrambling claws and landing on the ground again. This time he was furious, and he had no intention of giving up.

He ran out a ways from the boulder again, then turned, seeming very slow and deliberate in his movements. His eyes met Laman's with a fire that seemed to burn right through his head. Laman saw the beast's sides push out with a huge breath, and his eyes flickered. He was going to make his charge.

Without even thinking, only acting in terror, Laman had nocked an arrow and drawn back his bowstring. With deadly accuracy, before the lion could start its run, he let the arrow fly. The projectile flew true, and it sank up to its fletchings in the lion's chest. He leaped up into the air, landing with a loud growl and snapping at his chest with his great teeth.

Laman nocked another arrow, which once it flew would leave him only eight.

By this time, the three lionesses and the cubs had gone out about thirty more yards from the male lion and stood huddled and watching the strange creature on the rock that could reach out with its tiny weapons and hurt them so.

The big male made another rush toward Laman, but he seemed very weak, and he almost slammed into the face of the rock. Blinking his eyes and shaking his head as if to clear it, he went back by Naomi, then ran again. This time he veered off at the last second, growling low in his throat.

He would not look up toward Laman, as if not wanting to make eye contact. He limped back out to his starting place and tried to make another run, but came to a confused halt again a few yards out from the rock and raised his great, shaggy head, staring not up at the tiny man standing above him, the man who had dared to challenge his authority, but out at the sand. It was as if to look at the man now was to admit that Laman worried him, and he must know he was the greatest of beasts in this wilderness. No challenger was worthy to fight him. Few would dare find out.

Laman watched the big lion, and he dared not look at his Naomi, who sat so still on the desert sand, her blood and her hide on the ground all about her. The lion, even standing still, was growing weak and starting to waver, weaving from side to side.

A minute passed when suddenly the great beast turned away without looking again at Laman or the camel he had almost won and started walking with head low toward his females. Once, his lean hindquarters started to buckle sideways, but he managed to catch himself.

He started on, Laman watching him, and when he reached his females and the cubs, they all started off together, one of the females looking back toward the camel only once. Finally, one of the cubs, having no understanding why they had abandoned their evening meal, turned and sat on its haunches, staring back at Naomi with big amber eyes.

The other lions walked on, and some two hundred yards away Laman saw the great lion slump and fall. The lionesses gathered around him as he raised his huge hairy head and gave out a pitiful roar. Both lionesses started roaring, talking to the desert sky. Laman could barely hear the next groan that came from the male, and then his head went down and did not rise again.

With his wounded foot throbbing, Laman clambered down off the rock, his heart pounding with worse pain than that of his foot or his tailbone. With his bow still clutched tight, and the arrow nocked to it, he came around the rock. His eyes were fixed on the distant lions, gazing straight past his Naomi. But he could not long ignore her.

As he limped to his camel, she tried to rise, and he spoke to her softly. "Rise not, girl. Stay down." His words did not matter, and she tried again to come to her feet. But her leg bone was shattered, and the tendons at the back of it shredded and torn in half.

Laman eased around his camel, went to her face and fell on his knees, dropping his bow. Naomi looked at him through pitiful eyes, eyes that seemed much like those of a human now, for they were full of moisture, and tears had leaked down her cheeks.

He scratched her head and spoke soft words to her. He did not contemplate it and the sound surprised him when it came, but of a sudden he found himself singing her a song. It was a song he had learned long ago from his father, on one of their journeys up into Damascus.

Oh great ship of the desert,
My tower on the desert sand,
Greatest ship of the desert,
Bound for the Promised Land.

Oh great ship of the desert,
You have carried me afar,
Seen me through the storms of sand,
Led by a distant star.

Your milk has been my salvation,
You comforted with your gaze.
Now you part on your last journey
Where the camel angels graze.

Laman tried to see his Naomi, but his eyes were too full of tears. He glanced around, trying to see any sign of his cohorts or of their camels, but it was only him and Naomi. He stood up and circled her, surveying the damage. Her left haunch was shredded to the hip bone. And the tendons of that rear leg had been cut in half as well. His girl would never rise again, and she had lost much blood, but Naomi would not soon die, not on her own. She would wait here, in fear and loneliness after he left her, for whatever animals might come in time—the jackals, the wolves, perhaps a desperate leopard, hyenas, or maybe only the birds—the buzzards, the eagles, the ravens. And if not them, it would be the flies and the insects of the desert, and her flanks would swarm with maggots while she yet lived, and while she suffered alone, maybe wondering where Laman had gone, and why he had abandoned her here, and when he would return.

And wondering why she was powerless to rise.

Tears streamed down Laman's face as he unfastened her cinch and pulled the saddle from her, laying it in the sand. He gently removed her bridle too, and hardly able to see what he was doing he drew his knife from its sheath. It slipped from his fingers as he fell to his knees once more before his baby, his camel he had adopted some twenty years ago, had nursed with a bottle long after she was supposed to have been weaned.

Lehi would have been angry with him, for camel's milk was a valuable commodity, but Naomi had cried for it so. He remembered when he could still nearly pick her up, when she would come running to him on her wobbly legs and want to have her head and her ears scratched, and she would nuzzle his mouth, looking for the treats he usually had with him.

Naomi laid her head across the shoulder of her master—her *friend*. She rested her chin there, and Laman could no longer see.

He raised his hand and fondled her furry face, and she grunted at him in pleasure. And then, with his one hand on her face, he fumbled in the sand for his knife...

With shocked eyes, Shedrar and Lemuel surveyed the scene at the bottom of the mountain. They had been unsuccessful in their hunt, although Lemuel had foolishly expended one fine arrow on a small feral goat that was running. If only he had been as industrious as Laman in shooting blunted arrows at his father's innocent tame goats back home, perhaps he would have been a better marksman.

They came down out of the rocks, looking about them in bewilderment. Where three camels had been, there was nothing but Laman and the now-dead Naomi, who had shed a horrifying amount of blood in the sand. Laman sat in the sand, leaning against her side. His saddle lay on the ground with the bridle, several feet away.

Laman stared through his brother and brother-in-law, and finally his eyes came to focus on them.

"Lions," he said, and with great effort, due to the stiffening of his foot, he stood up with a hard look on his face. "The stupid animal couldn't figure out it was smarter to run away with the others than to stay here and play."

He turned away and made a show of looking out across the desert. Finally, he pointed out where the big lion lay. The females and cubs were lying down with him, but as Laman approached them, trying not to show his limp, they got up and trotted lightly off to the east, and he walked all the way out to the dead king.

The male lion did not look so big now, in his posture of death, with his eyes open to the sun and a trickle of blood staining the corner of his mouth. Viciously, Laman kicked him in the ribs, then with his knife bent down and sawed off the big feline's tail. It seemed an afterthought that made him crouch again as Shedrar and Lemuel watched, and painstakingly he removed all of the lion's claws and its upper and lower fangs and put them in his pouch.

Then he turned back to the others, clenching his jaw to make his face look hard and mean. "We have a long walk to tonight's camp, brothers. And a long walk to a draught of Ezion-geber wine. I killed an ibex that is lying up in the rocks past my stupid camel; we should at least go remove some of the meat and take it to camp with us."

"And how is your foot?" asked Shedrar. "Do you think you can actually walk all that way?"

"My foot is my bother," growled Laman. "I have had worse injuries wrestling with Nephi."

Lemuel laughed uneasily, not wanting to upset Laman. "Where is Ari? And Shedrar's camel?"

"Gone, of course. Most likely they followed the others on to camp—they saw which way they headed, and they can follow their scent. Camels aren't stupid. Except that cursed Naomi, perhaps."

Again he clenched his jaw and almost rushed past the two of them toward Naomi, to hide his face from them. He did not look down as he passed, but he did think of how grateful he was that Lemuel and Shedrar had not come down from the mountains any sooner than they had.

By the time Ishmael and the others reached their night's camp, the only place for another twenty miles that had any water, the old man was ailing badly. He could hardly keep his eyes open, and his face appeared gaunt, even though he had eaten whenever the others did. It was true that he ate little, and his body seemed somehow to be using up everything he took in and crying for more. His lips had cracked, but there was no blood.

Together, they set up their tents, and Ishmael went right away to lie down in his. Ra'ya came to Nephi, smiling fondly, and asked him to give her husband another blessing. Nephi put his hand on her shoulder. "I would be happy to do that, Ra'ya. I begin to wonder, though, what ails Ishmael. This lingering illness concerns me greatly."

Ra'ya tried to look brave, only nodding, and Nephi motioned for Sam and followed her back to their tent, which was the tent Nephi and his brothers had been using on their way to Jerusalem. Since the Bedouin had burned their big, exquisite tent, the brothers had given them theirs. Nephi would rather sleep under the stars anyway.

All of the daughters of Ishmael had gathered in the tent, and even Joab and Tikvah. Zipporah was nowhere to be seen, and Nephi feared that she was still openly mourning the death of her son and blaming Nephi for that death. The children were there also.

Bringing Sam to Ishmael's side with him, Nephi laid hands on the old man and waited for the Lord to tell him what to say. When the words began to come, they were not the words Nephi would have chosen were he to bless a sick person with words of his own.

"Ishmael son of She'alti'el," he began, "you are ailing with a strange disease we do not yet understand. Ishmael, beloved husband, father and friend, you will have comfort—comfort in knowing that you have those in your camp to look after your loved ones."

Here, Nephi's voice broke. The spirit was eerily quiet in speaking of Ishmael's actually being healed of this strange illness. This frightened Nephi, for in none of his blessings of the sick or hurt had this ever happened. Drawing a deep breath, he closed his eyes harder and went on.

"Ishmael, you have begat a strong progeny, a progeny that will go on, and some of whom will do high honor to your blessed name. At this time, you suffer greatly, and I bless you with the strength to withstand the pain and the suffering of the ills that rage inside you.

"Our Lord feels it imperative for you to know that this illness with which you now suffer is nothing to do with your worthiness before heaven. You have done no sin to bring this upon yourself. It is but a frailty, a sickness, of your advancing age.

"I also bless you with the knowledge that your wife will be strong and will be comforted by those around her, and she will be blessed with the ability to forgive and to stand strong in her convictions." He ended the blessing then as the voice of the Lord commanded him.

When he was finished, he raised his eyes slowly to Ra'ya. He feared what he would see in her face, yet he knew he had done no wrong. He had spoken the words of the Spirit which had come through the Lord. He had said nothing wrong, and he had left nothing out which should have been said. But would these people understand?

Ra'ya gazed up at him, trying to smile. But a question burned in her eyes. Nephi could feel everyone else staring at him as well, and as Ishmael continued to lie on his bed and did not rise, the tension inside the tent grew.

"Why, Nephi? Were you not able to bless him to rise and be healed, as you have done before? You can see that he needs this." Her eyes earnestly searched his, and without his feeling it her fingers had come out to lay on his forearm and squeeze it.

"Mother Ra'ya, I wish I could tell you. When a man humbly useth the Priesthood, it is not given that he should speak of himself, but only the words of the Lord. The Lord did not command me to tell Ishmael to be healed and to rise. I wanted to hear these words, and I wanted to say them. But the Lord did not grant me that power."

He searched her eyes, praying for her understanding. Instead, she just frowned and dropped her hand from his arm, crouching back down beside her husband.

With a great sadness on his shoulders, Nephi left the tent, and he heard others drift out behind him. Once outside the tent, they all went their separate directions, only a handful of them following Nephi—Lotan, Yona, Yael and Sam. Even Rachel did not come to him this time. Instead, she gathered with her sisters and brothers near where Joab was wordlessly building a fire.

Nephi turned to the others, knowing they sought answers of him. He only wished he had those answers to give.

"I have seen you heal people that were wounded unto death," said Lotan quietly. "Yet when you could have healed your own nephew, Jephthah, you allowed him to die. And now Ishmael you have left ailing as well. Please help me to understand."

The words almost brought tears to Nephi, for almost of all the people in camp, all but Sam, he would have expected Lotan to stand beside him. Then the Spirit spoke to him, whispered that indeed Lotan was only seeking understanding. He did not come to blame his friend.

Nephi waited as the others watched him, waited until he felt the strength of Sam's hand on his arm. There were words inside his heart that at this important moment he did not recognize as the Lord's or as his own. He only knew he must speak them.

"Lotan, my brother, prayer is given us for our use, as a tool and as a comfort. And blessings, although they call with more authority to our Lord because they call upon the name of his priesthood, are the same—a tool of great importance. But blessings—*true* blessings can only be spoken as the Lord sees fit. The Lord has reasons for everything he does, for everything he allows to happen or which he stops from happening.

"Mere mortals will never understand all of the Lord's ways, and I am no better than a mere mortal. If I had the power of myself, and if mere faith were enough, I would have spoken the words that would have healed Ishmael. But I was not allowed to do this.

"If this were the only thing we needed, then no one beloved would ever die. They would live to be thousands of years old, for the mere blessings of men, not God's will, would keep them alive, and hale. The Lord chooses a time for all great men to pass through the veil—Adam, Noah, Abraham, Joseph, Moses, David. No man, however great, however wise or however beloved, can remain on this earth forever, and we as mortals have no right to keep them here. Only God can choose this."

All of these people, even Nephi, were misty-eyed when he finished speaking. The spirit had spilled over the space around them so that everyone knew these words had not come from Nephi, but from the Lord. Without saying a word, Yael drew near and embraced Nephi, an embrace as a loving sister, the embrace of comfort he so needed at that moment.

Chapter Four

The Rescue

The camp where they had stopped had water, but only a small, dirty well some eight feet deep. The well would always refill itself, but slowly, and it was a long process watering all of the camels and the people too, when each camel might drink twenty-five gallons of water before completely replenished.

The campsite was not beautiful like some of the others they had seen, but water was water, and out in this forsaken land there was no choice. Still, there were a few trees around, and the oleander bushes that bloomed off and on, looking so pretty yet so deadly for the camels or any other animal that ate of their leaves, one or two of which might be fatal.

Nephi found himself looking now and then up the trail the way they had come, and it was nearing dark, with no sign of the hunters. The family of Ishmael kept to themselves, and Nephi did not visit their side of the camp, even to see Rachel. It was obvious that his failure to say any words to heal Ishmael had offended them, and it saddened him that they did not understand the ways of the Lord.

He felt that at least Ishmael, if he had been in his right mind, would tell them the truth, would counsel them about their feelings toward Nephi. But the old man seemed very sick, and whatever illness he was suffering truly frightened Nephi. To know that he was not allowed by the Lord to speak any healing words was worst of all.

The sun had sunk behind the mountains, and the purple desert sands waxed cool, when Nephi saw through the gloaming the two tall shapes swaying toward him. A camel on the run is not an animal some might imagine it to be. With its neck stretched out straight before it and its long legs pumping, it is really quite graceful. But these two shapes, two camels, were not beautiful to Nephi tonight, for both of them were rider-less.

Without saying anything to the others, Nephi ran out and met Ari and Shedrar's camel. Naomi was nowhere in sight. At first he assumed that Lemuel and Shedrar had been careless in tying them up, but the camels were too skittish for him to believe that. Ari rushed right by him, grunting fearfully and rolling his eyes. When he recognized it was Nephi past whom he had run he turned about, bawling, and came back to him, lowering his head.

"Ari, how come you here? Where is Lemuel?" asked Nephi softly, scratching Ari's shaggy head and rubbing his jaw. He moved around him slowly, his hands questing over his hide, and at his left haunch Nephi stopped when Ari flinched. Nephi raised his hand, which seemed to be wet, and sniffed at it. There was blood there.

Shedrar's camel had gone on past and must be with the rest of the herd by now. Two of Ishmael's dogs were barking, and one of the camels bawled, then had his complaint drowned out by Ari's roar. Unlike any other night, it was not a comical sound. Nephi shook his head and moved back up to Ari's face. "Easy, big Ari. My ears can only take so much."

He took the camel by the bridle, leading him toward the others, and as he walked Sam and Lotan came up to him. "Ari has been attacked, I think," said Nephi. "There is blood on his flank."

"Are the others not back then?" asked Sam.

"Not yet. But neither is Naomi."

"What will we do?" asked Lotan.

"I must make a torch and go after them," replied Nephi. "They might be hurt out there."

"You would go back there—in the dark? After all they have done and said to you?"

"They are my brothers."

For a moment Lotan was silent, pondering on this simplest of statements that said everything important about his friend Nephi. "Then I will go with you. And Sam, too."

Nephi started to protest, but then he realized he might need more help. There was no telling what he would find on the back-trail—that is if he found anything at all before sunup.

"Then we must go now. They are weary, but we will take Ari and Shedrar's camel, because they will know where to go."

"They are very skittish," said Sam. "Are you certain?"

"Their fear will tell us when we are near."

And so Nephi saddled Abraham while Sam saddled Chakir, and Lotan put his saddle and bridle on one of the other camels. Nephi and his family had had the foresight to collect much pitch from the pine trees that grew in the hills around Jerusalem, and with this pitch and a stout branch he made himself a torch. He would not light it until the need was dire, so as not to draw the attention of any wandering desert marauder, but it would be a comfort to have when they drew near to where the camels had been left tied.

Telling the others what had happened, Nephi and his partners started back up the trail, leading Ari and Shedrar's beast.

The desert, so like a furnace during the day, can feel like winter in the night, particularly when a wind commences to blow.

One of those winds picked up tonight, and although it was no-where near the sandstorm that had beset them before, it was plenty to whip them with sand and make them wish they were under shelter back in camp.

The desert sank to deepest black, and the coolness of it made it smell like a different place than where they had traveled in the day. They could see the black humps of mountains shouldered against the ice-chipped black of the sky, and a smoky gilded moon rose full and bold in the east.

To Nephi, riding near the feet of the sloping, rock-hewn moun-tains, he felt all of the magic of his childhood tales of ghouls and monsters, ogres, and of course the giants, who were huge and fe-rocious and sometimes cannibalistic, who in the words of Moses's spies made men feel like grasshoppers.

These mountain crags must teem with all of these and with haunting spirits, if any place in the world did. The winds screamed across the boulder tops, moaned in the gullies, strummed evil mu-sic in the branches of the acacia trees. Even at his age, Nephi could not help but feel a sense of trepidation here in this merciless land, now so dark and forbidding.

They had traveled only three and a half miles when Nephi heard voices, and he drew Abraham to a halt. Sam and Lotan grouped around him in confusion until they, too, heard the voices, and then all was still. Nephi wanted to light his torch, but instead his hand went to his sword, Elnathan. "Who is there?"

"I, Laman!" came the answer after a moment. "And Lemuel and Shedrar. Nephi, is that you?"

"Yes! With Sam and Lotan." Nephi made his camel lie down, and the others followed suit, all clambering off their mounts.

Nephi ran toward the sound of sandals in the gravel, and he spoke Laman's name again. Then his brother was there, and for a moment he was hesitant, but Nephi threw his arms around him.

"What happened? Are you all right?"

"We are fine," replied Laman, waiting for Lemuel and Shedrar to catch up.

Lemuel got there, and Nephi hugged him too, although the embrace in return was not very warm. Both brothers threw their arms around Sam as well, and Sam laughed with relief.

"Lions came," said Laman. "They chased Shedrar's camel and Ari away. Ari! Some lion he turned out to be!" said Laman, jokingly.

But Nephi could tell he was hiding something and he intuited that on this night the darkness was Laman's ally. He hated to ask, but he had to. "Laman... Where is Naomi?"

"That stupid animal did not run like the others," said Laman, his voice husky. "She was growing useless anyway. So Nephi, I must ask... Why did you come for us?"

Although Nephi knew for certain now that Laman needed the darkness to hide his pain, for he knew how deeply he had loved Naomi, he wished he could see his face as they spoke. It would have meant so much more to see that he still had loving emotions in his eyes.

"Laman, I love you. You are my brother. I could not but come for you."

He felt his big brother's strong hand come out and clap him on the shoulder, and Laman choked out words that sounded like gibberish. Out of mercy, Nephi did not ask him to repeat it.

"It took you a long time to come," said Shedrar from the darkness. "When did our camels return?"

Sam's voice in reply was terse. "What? Nephi took time only to fashion a torch. We came as fast as we could—and it was Nephi who planned it, without even asking for me and Lotan to accompany him."

Shedrar only made a quiet grunt to this, and after a moment he said, "Did you bring back my camel, too?"

"Yes, we brought your camel," said Sam dully.

Nephi was glad his brother spoke, for he was too disappointed in Shedrar to talk to him at that moment.

"Are any of you hurt?" Nephi asked Laman. "How did you chase away the lions?"

"The male I killed," said Laman, digging a fang out of his pouch and pressing it into Nephi's hand. "One arrow in the chest. The others simply left. And we have meat, too. We have each carried a large portion of an ibex."

Without saying more, Laman limped away, and soon he came back lugging one of the hair-covered hindquarters of the ibex. He bade Nephi hold out his hands and then laid across them the heavy, meaty tail of the lion. "That, the fangs and his claws are my trophies in exchange for the death of my camel." His voice broke on the last word, and Nephi shuddered at the weight of the fuzzy tail across his hands. He no longer wished to see the emotion in his brother's face. It was mercy for both of them that he did not. Also, he had seen the very noticeable limp his brother affected now, and he couldn't dredge up the courage to ask how bad was the wound that caused it.

They picked up the other two loads of meat and lashed them on the backs of the camels. Lemuel was stroking Ari's neck and speaking soft words to him when Nephi stopped beside him.

"We came as soon as we could, brother," he said softly, hoping Shedrar would not hear.

"It was good to hear your voice, Nephi," said Lemuel. "It was never better. I... wondered if you would come."

Nephi put his big arm around Lemuel's neck. "I would die before I would let you perish alone in the wilderness. You should never forget that."

In the darkness, Nephi saw his brother nod. He seemed unable to speak.

They rode in silence all the way back to camp. Even Laman did not speak, for the courage he had been able to summon upon the arrival of his rescuers had ebbed and gone, and he was left with an empty heart and searing pains in his foot and tailbone.

They quietly bedded their camels and climbed off, then brushed them down and gave them water and fed them. Lemuel, who was not so attached to Ari as Laman had been to Naomi, went to camp to start cooking hunks of meat from the ibex. As for Laman, he stayed long with the camel herd, stroking Ari quietly while the beast made a sound like a gargling purr.

At the fire, the smell of the roasting ibex flesh began to rise into the air, and it was a welcome scent. The family of Ishmael was gathered there, and because of the warmth Lotan and Yona soon gravitated to it as well, with Yael trailing along with them because she was paired with no one. Even Sam, after speaking with Nephi long enough to ascertain his feelings, making sure that Nephi would not feel slighted, finally went to sit on the ground at the fire.

The dry wood, its heat augmented by camel droppings, made white-orange flames dance straight up in the darkness, flickering and leaping, shooting their light out to illuminate the faces that stared into them, mesmerized. From a distance, Nephi watched, wishing in one way that he could be with the others, but knowing he was set apart from them, especially this night.

He wanted to tell them not to make a habit of staring into the flames, in case they were set upon by marauders, but he knew he had overstepped his bounds too many times, and this was not a battle he could win or was willing to fight. Let Lehi tell them, for in time he certainly would. Any wise traveler of the wastelands knew better than to burn his eyes by the fire and blind himself to shadows that might attack from the dark. It was dangerous even to have the fire at all, but in time Lehi would tell them that, too, as was his place as the patriarch.

Before long, Laman came limping into camp carrying several wineskins. Nephi noticed the fearsome looking wounds on Laman's foot, and it wasn't hard to guess what had caused them. He wanted to offer to boil some salt water to bathe them, then dress them with olive oil and linen. But it was obvious that Laman did not want any attention paid to them right now. And anyway, perhaps more important at the moment was the wine Laman was carrying.

Nephi had seen the two casks on Laman's pack camel that he and the others had purchased during their night in Ezion-geber, and he knew it was from these casks they were refilling their skins. Worry crept into his heart, for this night of all nights, with Nephi's failure to heal Ishmael and the death of Laman's beloved camel, the wine would not be a friend to anyone.

Of a merry heart, wine can make a merrier, but where shadows loom in the soul, wine will make darkness grow on the tongue.

The wine started going around the circle, and Nephi could not look away. From his place in the darkness, with morbid curiosity, he watched for the transformation he had seen so many times. This time, even before the wine began its evil labors, the tongues began to loosen.

Ze'eva told Shedrar, Laman and Lemuel about what she referred to as Nephi's "refusal" to heal Ishmael. For a few moments there was silence, but then Shedrar said, "Without the evil spirits of the Bedouin about, perhaps his black magic has no power."

There were a few laughs around the fire. It saddened Nephi to see that one came from his brother Laman, and Lemuel laughed, of course because of Laman. "Perhaps he was used up," suggested Joab. "It must take a toll on someone to use his priesthood power to heal six dying people."

Shedrar started to laugh. Nephi could see his face better than most of the others, for he sat directly across from him. But when no one else laughed, Shedrar quieted down, gazing at his older brother. Perhaps he had suddenly realized Joab was serious.

The drinking went on, coupled with long periods of heavy silence. After a while, Ari'el looked around her at the darkness, and seeming not to see whatever she was looking for she said in a low voice, "Sam, why do you really suppose Nephi would not bless Father? Were those desert people worth so much more, after all Father has done for Nephi?"

Sam looked around the fire, his eyes filled with shame and sadness. "I am surprised to hear this question. Nephi has done so much for all of us. He has risked his life for us, he has done his best to keep us safe from what will surely befall Jerusalem. He cannot tell you why he was directed to utter the words of blessing that he did. That is the Lord's choice, not Nephi's, who can only use the Lord's priesthood to speak words that are given to him. Your own father would tell you the same, and I am surprised that he hasn't."

Shedrar laughed loudly, as did several of his brothers. Sadly, Nephi saw that Laman and Lemuel laughed again as well, but not with as much conviction as the others.

"Do you truly believe those words, Sam?" Shedrar asked. "Has Nephi convinced you too that he is a mighty prophet of God?"

After staring at Shedrar for some time, Sam said, "Never have I doubted it. And how can you have seen the same things I did in our camp the night the Bedouin came and yet not believe that he *does* have the power of God inside him?"

Shedrar took a long swig of wine and made a point of swallowing slowly, then belching. It was almost as if he were stalling while he struggled to summon a reply.

"I do not know what I truly saw that night, Sam. A trick of the mind. A trick of Baal-zebub. I know not. But I do not believe it was the power of God."

Lotan suddenly stood up, the light of the fire washing over him. "You cannot tell me you did not feel the power in that camp, Shedrar. Surely, you cannot be that blind. I saw the tears on your cheeks—just like on everyone else's."

Slowly, Shedrar got up, putting his hand to his short sword. "You should learn your place as a guest in our camp, boy. You never should have been here in the first place. Your crime in Ezion-geber might well have cost us our lives. You had no right to ask to come with us, and Nephi had no right to allow it, especially without asking our leave. If you do not learn to keep your mouth shut, then I will shut it for you."

"I will *not* keep my mouth shut," said Lotan levelly. "For you, Shedrar, act the fool."

Before Shedrar could move, Nephi was standing at the edge of the firelight, looking mighty and fierce and somewhat like the giants of old, with the scarlet flame-light flickering over his angry features.

"Shedrar!" he barked, seeing Shedrar start to pull his sword from its sheath. "If you wish to fight, then you will fight with me. But I do not ask for battle. I ask only for peace."

"Shedrar," said Laman suddenly, as if embarrassed to learn that Nephi had been listening to their conversation, "you have to admit that Nephi did come out to find us tonight when he did not have to. I question whether you, or even I, would have gone out into the dark wilderness to find him. Can you not at least grant him peace this one night, if only for that?"

"So he wanted to see if we had any meat!" Shedrar said derisively. "Hunger can drive a man to do strange things."

Lemuel laughed, but Laman's face remained serious. Laman turned his eyes and stared into the depths of the fire. "You are right that he should not have brought Lotan and Yona into our midst without telling us what happened, but it is no reason to fight him. Besides, in your place I would not be so certain who would win."

Shedrar growled something unintelligible, then plopped back down on the ground. "Your brother is a big, stupid oaf who desires to be our king. The only place he would lead us is to destruction."

Nephi did not need to trade harsh words with these people, so he walked away. After he had gone, unbeknownst to him, Rachel and Ari'el also got up and left to bed down in their tent. Sam, Lotan, Yona and Yael also deserted the fire. If there was any roasted meat left when the drinkers of the wine were finished, perhaps they would partake. For now, it was too hot where the meat was roasting, and the heat was not all from the fire.

Nephi lay on the sand at the base of a stunted palm tree and listened to the sounds of the merry-making at the fire. It grew louder and louder, and the voices there more and more derisive. Most of the talk, of course, was from Shedrar, Hidai, Gera and Yavin, and was of Nephi, but the words that hurt perhaps the most were spoken of his friends, Lotan, Yona and Yael, and his brother Sam. The wine was creating its own thoughts and words, and when alcohol thinks there is no word of wisdom to quell the insanity of its logic. Nephi only listened so that he could learn the true secrets of what lurked in these people's hearts. One thing he knew for certain: Wine, whether speaking good or speaking evil, always speaks the heart.

But then he thought back to Laman standing up for him, and for one solitary moment his heart was warmed.

Chapter Five

Rebellion!

Nephi finally drifted off, but by then he had heard from his party both harsh humor and unbridled anger, all at his expense and at the expense of those who believed in him and his father. The humor was always cutting, just on the edge of anger, and always it turned to anger before it turned to other subjects.

And by now, the wine and the bad spirit at the fire had taken over everyone, for even Laman's words had turned once more to anger, and he had forgotten how he was defending Nephi earlier for coming out in the dark to search for the lost hunters.

There was talk of how Naomi had been gravely wounded and Laman had had to put her out of her misery, which never would have happened had they not been drawn out of their home on false pretenses. They spoke of how Nephi had allowed Jephthah to die, and possibly now Ishmael would die as well, yet Nephi had been willing and more than able to heal the Bedouin people, who were complete strangers—assuming this had not been merely a trick of the devil.

Everything bad, and nothing good that had happened since leaving Jerusalem was directly attributed to Nephi, and not the least of the problem was how he lorded it over the other men in camp, every one of which rightly should have enjoyed leadership over him.

Nephi's heart ached. After all the things he had done, after saving his family and friends from sure destruction by the raiders, after endangering himself by going into the dark after Laman, Lemuel and Shedrar, all they could do was speak against him. He knew it was the wine talking now, yet the thoughts had been lurking in their minds already. The wine only brought them to the surface. For a little time he had thought Laman might have changed in his heart, but that time had passed.

Nephi slept, and his slumber was restless. Late into the night he heard the guttural roaring of lions. But he no longer cared. There were moments he thought it would be far easier if one of them came and dragged him away for its breakfast. Yet of course that was not to be the case, and while the lions kept their distance Nephi slept on.

In the morning, in spite of the restless night, Nephi got up in the earliest gray light and walked the rounds of the camp. All were asleep now, many of them sprawled about the dead fire in their drunkenness. For a long moment Nephi stood looking down at Laman. His brother had once been his hero, so big and brave and strong—all that he had hoped to grow up to be.

His face had a dark cast to it, low and heavy of brow, narrow of eye, and sharp of nose, his mouth slightly down-turned by nature, even when he was not frowning of himself. Yet Laman was a handsome man, and charming in his way, and there was more than one young maiden in Jerusalem who would have been happy to have her father and Lehi pair them together. Laman looked so peaceful in his sleep. Nephi longed to sit down by him and reminisce, recall the good times of their childhood, when life seemed so easy and free.

Then there was Lemuel. Lemuel had always been the easier going of his two older brothers. Yet in spite of that, Nephi had never felt the bond between them that he once had with Laman. Far back when Laman had doted on Nephi, then Lemuel had seemed somehow jealous of him. And now that Laman's normal desire seemed to be belittling or deriding Nephi, Lemuel was more than happy to follow suit, laughing at Laman's jokes, making a stab of his own whenever he saw a good opening.

Now, in his sleep, Lemuel was like Laman, peaceful, not unpleasant to look upon, with a face Nephi remembered fondly and loved. Lemuel's was a slightly softer face than Laman's, not so hard in its lines, nor so low of brow, yet every bit as dark of eye and sharp of nose. His skin also bragged the same deep tan color. But every dark aspect of Lemuel's face vanished when he smiled or laughed, for a light seemed to brighten his visage, and if the smile was genuine there was a soft, affectionate spark in his eyes that could melt Nephi's heart.

Thirdly, Nephi contemplated Shedrar. For almost as long as he could remember, Shedrar had taken pleasure in tormenting him. He had never shown any open liking for him, and the best Nephi could remember from him was disdain and apathy. Nephi said this of few men, but he had come to dislike his brother-in-law and to pity his little sister for having married the man. And it was a horrible shame, for Tikvah was one of the most beautiful, loving, and giving women Nephi had ever known, a far greater gift than Shedrar would ever deserve.

Joab, the oldest of the Ishmael children, was still a puzzle to Nephi. He often seemed to be riding a wall, drifting between wanting to love Nephi and wanting to follow Shedrar on his road of hatred. Joab had once thought highly of Nephi, and they had shared some good laughs. Nephi hoped they still shared some of the same fond memories. Now, in this time of trial, Joab still seemed somewhat softer toward his brother-in-law than even his own brothers, Laman and Lemuel. But since Nephi had not been able to bless Ishmael to be healed, Nephi greatly feared that had changed.

With satisfaction, he noticed that the sons of Ishmael's dead brother, Neriah and Eran, had both gone to their own tents. But Ishmael's daughters, Ze'eva and Yaakova, were still at the remains of the fire with the men, and since Ra'ya was so upset about Ishmael's condition she had not come out to keep an eye on them or make them go to their tent. Both women had consumed far too much wine, and from the looks of it Yaakova had thrown up near the big log on which she had been seated. He crouched by her and watched her throat for a pulse before he moved on. She had made cutting comments about him in her drunkenness during the night, yet he would have been grieved to learn she had choked to death on her own vomitus.

With a sigh, Nephi straightened up and moved on about camp. He could hear loud snores inside the tent of Ishmael, where most of the children were sleeping inside one of the two partitions. The snores he recognized as Ishmael's, so his father's old friend was still alive, and that made Nephi happy. He just prayed they could swiftly get the old man to Lehi, for if anyone could help him it would be he.

The huge herd of camels was standing about peacefully, a few of them grazing, and the dogs sat quietly by them, their ears pricked and their eyes studying the half-dark. The sounds of the lions were too recent for them to let down their guard. But looking beyond camp, Nephi could see no sign that the lions had remained near. All was quiet, and the purple-gray, dawn-lit sand and gravel stretched on out to the foot of the distant mountains, where at the ridgeline the sky was fanning silver.

Nephi went back to where he had slept and girded his sword about his loins. Then he picked up his bow, slung his quiver of arrows across his back, and set out away from camp. He really did not intend to hunt. The purpose of his weapons was more one of self-defense, but if he saw an oryx or anything that might be of use later, and was within range, neither would he refuse the Lord's bounty.

Half a mile from camp, in the smallest of the foothills of the barren mountains rising overhead, he knelt in prayer. He asked for guidance, and he asked for mercy. He asked for patience with his brothers and with the family of Ishmael, who were angry with him. He begged for tolerance, and thanked the Lord for his abundant love, and the friendship of those in camp who were ever-faithful.

Nephi felt a warm presence all around him, even in the cold of the breaking dawn. The eastern sky was pinking now, and that rosy glow crept over the sand and the mountain faces in the west. The eastern range, below the approaching sun, was still hazy and purple, and the lightening sky was empty of cloud.

Gladness and peace filled his heart as he stood up from his prayer, and he took in a deep breath of the cool desert air. The smell of it was bracing, pure, a smell that could be compared to no other, and certainly beat the stench of the city, where human and animal wastes, unless someone buried them, had nowhere to be thrown but beside the houses and in the streets, to be washed away only in the event of a rare rain.

God had intended people to live this way, with the land, not stacked into filthy cities like so much cordwood. For all Jerusalem's glory and beauty, the true beauty of God's creations was manifest in his open spaces, his mountains, valleys and deserts, where the air was swept clean by wind, washed by rain and dried by the sun, and all that was here was of nature.

Walking back to camp, feeling much refreshed, both spiritually and physically, Nephi hoped to see tents being struck. But nothing had changed. The intoxicated still slept by the fire pit, and the camels still wandered free. Even Sam and Lotan, Neriah, Eran and the faithful women slept, but Nephi could not really blame them. Those at the fire had made sleep fitful and rest hard to obtain for everyone in camp.

Gently, Nephi roused Sam and Lotan, and with regret he woke Yael and Yona. He could not bring himself to disturb the daughters of Ishmael in their tent, however, so he let them sleep for now. But he stood there beside the tent and listened to the inner silence, wishing Rachel would talk to him, wishing she could understand why he had not been able to bless her father with the words she and her mother had desired.

Last of all, Nephi went to his older brothers, and he stood staring at them for a long time, wishing he could put off their wakening. But he was looking forward to seeing his mother and father, Elnathan and Zoram and the others, and if they were to have an easy journey this last day they would have to begin early.

He crouched and shook Laman's shoulder, speaking softly. "Laman, wake up. We have to strike camp and prepare for our journey. Laman?"

Groggy, his brother opened one eye, putting up a hand to ward off the pale gray of the sky. "Wha—? What are you doing, Nephi? It is still night."

Nephi laughed. "It is morning, brother, and tonight we come by the sea and meet Father and Mother, who wait for us."

Laman blinked hard, cramming his eyes shut against the light. Rolling over, he grumbled, "Go away, Nephi. A few more minutes of sleep."

Nephi crouched for a moment longer, then moved on to Lemuel, trying the same gentle tactics with him, to no better effect.

Finally, Nephi let out a sigh and went back to Laman. Drawing in a new breath, he took him by the shoulder and shook him much more roughly. "Laman, get up. We have to be moving."

By now, Nephi could hear that even in the tent of Ishmael's daughters they were moving around, and there were sounds in Ishmael's tent. These at the fire were going to end up being the last awake—the men, sleeping drunk by the fire while the women tried to do all the work.

Laman looked up at Nephi again, his eyes only slits. The look was dark. "I will rise when I rise, Nephi. Get your hand off me."

"I won't get my hand off you, brother, not until you get up and go to work. There is too much to do."

"My head hurts."

"Yes, I suppose it does. Too much wine only pretends in the night to be your friend—and you drank too much wine."

Laman grabbed Nephi's hand and flung it away from him, coming up onto his knees. "Go away from me. I will not tell you again."

Seeing that Laman was not only very irate but was already partly up, Nephi moved back to Lemuel. He was too disgruntled himself to think any more about being gentle, so instead of crouching down he nudged Lemuel with his foot. "Get up, Lemuel. It is time to face the day."

It was not Lemuel's but Shedrar's voice that came in reply, from across the fire. "Get away from us, Nephi, before something you do not like happens to you. You are not our master."

Nephi instantly regretted Shedrar's having come awake while he was near, and especially in this manner. But that could not be helped now.

"Your sisters are stirring and will soon be dressed and moving. Would you like everyone else to think of you as children, while the women do your work?"

Shedrar staggered to his feet, sand falling off him. With one large red wrinkle all the way across the left side of his face, even over his eye, from sleeping with the material of his tunic between his face and his arm, and with dried spittle all down the side of his mouth, Shedrar looked silly. But the look in his eyes was deadly. "You are the child, Nephi, and a fool of a child at that. You are going to push me too far, and I will not be responsible for what happens to you."

"Easy, Shedrar," came Joab's voice. He had sat up, his hair sticking in all directions, and was looking at his younger brother through bleary eyes. "The women are about."

Shedrar whirled on Joab. "Does that matter? Nephi speaketh of us before the women, treats us like stupid little children—so why not do the same to him?"

Joab gave a little shrug and looked up at Nephi. There was little he could say to that, for he had felt the same way himself at times. In spite of this, he rose to his feet and brushed off his clothing, then walked around and woke up his cousins who were still at the fire. Next, he went and gently woke Ze'eva and Yaakova. The women came up quickly and walked to their tent. As they arrived, the others were filing out.

Zipporah had come to the fire site now, walking deliberately far away from Nephi to circle the bed of embers and stop near her husband.

"Are you all right, Zipporah? How did you sleep?" asked Nephi.

Zipporah's eyes flashed up at him. "I did *not* sleep, Nephi! Thank you. My son has died. I am mourning. My own brother forsook his nephew—my son—then healed six people we did not even know. I am *not* all right, and you obviously do not care, so do not ask. In fact, I would prefer that you did not speak to me at all."

"Zipporah, I want to talk to you," countered Nephi. "Please come with me."

"Get away from me, Nephi!" Zipporah screamed. "Go!"

Nephi started to walk around the clearing to her, and Joab jumped forward and shoved him back. "Get away, Nephi. Do not come near my wife. Did you not hear her?"

Shedrar jumped into the conflict of a sudden. "And let us talk about those six people you saved, Nephi, since we are talking. Without asking our leave, you appointed yourself master of this family, and you made an agreement with the sheikh to heal them. It was on pain of death for Hagith, two of our men, and the taking of all the women as slaves—or worse. Who do you think you are? You have endangered this family for the last time. I, for one, am going back to Jerusalem."

The words dropped like a large rock in a still pond. Everyone in camp with the exception of Ishmael was standing around watching the building altercation, and so all heard Shedrar's harsh voice.

"We are going too," said Laman. "Enough of this travel in the wilderness. I do not care if I never see my father again. He is a complete fool. I am going back to the land of my inheritance."

Hidai, Gera, Yavin, Ze'eva and Yaakova were in agreement, and they spoke angry words at Nephi that in his confusion hardly even registered on him.

"We will also go," agreed Zipporah. "Jerusalem shall stand strong. This the Lord hath promised of old."

Hearing these words come from his beloved sister, Nephi stepped over to appeal to her. "Please, Zipporah, don't do this!"

"The decision is made, Nephi," growled Laman. "And you are not welcome to come back with us even if you wanted to. Go down to Father by the sea. The land of promise is all yours."

"Laman! Lemuel!" Nephi said pleadingly. "You are my older brothers. How can you be so hard in your hearts and blind in your minds that you need me, your younger brother, always to set an example for you?"

"An example! An example of *what?*" barked Lemuel. "Of the greatest fool alive? Or should I say second greatest? I am not sure, for it is between you and our father."

"How can you not listen to the Lord's voice?" Nephi pleaded. "Have you forgotten that you saw an angel, the same as Sam and I did? Look at all of the ways the Lord has blessed us, in delivering us out of the hands of Laban, and also the Bedouin, and in allowing us to receive the records of the earth and of our fathers.

"Brothers, let us be faithful! Do not go back to Jerusalem when you know as well as I that you will be destroyed there!"

"You know nothing of this!" Shedrar barked. "You tell us these lies of the devil so that you might take us all away from our homeland and so that you might try to be made a ruler over us, all of whom should be *your* leader, by the rights of age."

"I *do* know, Shedrar. If we are faithful we shall obtain a land of promise. And in time ye shall know of the destruction of Jerusalem, as great as she might now seem. As you know, the spirit of the Lord ceaseth to strive with those in Jerusalem, for the Jews have rejected the prophets, and as you have already seen they have cast Jeremiah into prison! Also, they have sought to take away the life of our father."

"And perhaps they should have taken it," said Laman harshly. "He is but a fool—a thorn in our sides."

Nephi took in a deep breath, trying to control his anger. "All right, Laman. If you wish to go, then go ye up to Jerusalem. And when you lie dying in your blood or are a captive of the Chaldeans, remember the words I spoke unto you, the words which the Lord constraineth me to speak. As for you, Shedrar, I did not ask to be your leader. I would that you might follow the spirit of the Lord, that we all might live in peace together. It is the Lord who has told me that I should lead this family, because of the iniquity of my elder brothers. I wish—"

He never got to finish his sentence, for suddenly with such ferocity and speed that Nephi could not avoid it, Zipporah struck him across the face with her open hand. "Stop, Nephi! Just stop talking!" She slapped him again, and again, before he grabbed her wrist.

A sharp blow from where Joab stood crashed across Nephi's shoulders, striking hard on his spine. Pain shot all throughout his body, and everything went white. He dropped to his knees, and people swarmed all over him like ants on a wounded bee.

Chapter Six

The Homecoming

When Nephi started to come back to his senses, he could feel that he was trussed up, unable to move, and he was being lugged by the arms and by the feet. After a time, he was dropped like a sack, and he hit the ground hard, the breath driven from him as if he had been kicked in the stomach by a camel. In another moment strong hands grasped him, and he felt himself lifted off the ground once more.

In the back of his conscious he could hear voices screaming, the voice of Sam, and also of Lotan. And there were women's voices, too. Shedrar yelled back at them, along with Laman, Lemuel and Joab, and some of Ishmael's nephews. Nephi was only half aware of what was going on around him, so harsh had the blow fallen on his spine. His head lolled down, and he felt like he was going to vomit.

After a few minutes, he could no longer hear the plaintive voices, but now he heard Shedrar say something about "this being a good place," and they threw him down on the ground, little rocks biting into his flesh. After the fall, he lay there and could hardly breathe. It felt like someone was sitting on his back.

"You can stay here and be devoured by the wild beasts, Nephi," came Laman's harsh voice. "The way Naomi was butchered because you brought us here. You are a curse on our people, and we are going home."

Groggily, Nephi tried to open his eyes and see where he was. But he was lying on his belly, just barely starting to get back the breath that had been knocked from him when he fell, and he could only listen to the retreating footsteps. When he breathed, dust and sand snuffed into his nostrils, choking him.

Before long, in the distance, he could hear more yelling and screaming, but the voices were unintelligible. Women were crying, and a man began to say something loudly but then seemed to be stilled by force. He half expected to soon be joined here by Sam and Lotan, also trussed up, but for a long time he heard no other sounds.

In time, Nephi could hear the voices of the camels, but there was little human sound. Of people the world seemed eerily void. Nephi lay there and breathed, trying to keep from choking on the dust and sand in his face. He struggled with the bands on his feet and hands, but whoever had tied these knots was serious. There would be no escaping these ropes.

If someone like Sam or Lotan or one of the women did not come for him, Nephi would die here. It seemed so easy that Laman and Lemuel, his own flesh and blood, were pushed over the edge to murder their brother. But they must have been building up to this for some time. He had been blind!

He wrenched at the bands again, tore at them until it felt like his hands and feet would bleed, for the fiber of which the ropes were made was very stiff and prickly. At last, he lay there, trying to think.

Because he was Nephi, his first thoughts were of the Lord. He did not have to remain here tied up at all!

"Oh, Lord," he prayed, "according to my faith which is in Thee, wilt Thou deliver me from the hands of my brethren? Give me strength that I may burst these bands with which I am bound."

He had no more than spoken the words and had not again tested the cords tied so tightly around him, when he felt the pressure leave his wrists and his ankles. He tried to move, only to find that the bands had fallen away and were lying loose on the ground. There had been a time Nephi might have been astounded, but he knew even as he prayed that the Lord would deliver him. He gave a prayer of thanks, and then he stood, took a deep breath, and walked back to the camp, all caution flown from him. He was under the protection of the Lord!

As he approached, he could see that Sam and Lotan were with the camels, and Shedrar was standing near them holding a length of rope as if it were a whip. Both Hidai and Yavin also stood nearby. The women were meekly wrapping food and folding tents, and in the camp there was no sound of human voice. A horrible tension rose up from these people that was almost tactile.

Then Nephi saw Joab's daughter, Hagith, point toward him and yell, "Nephi is coming!"

Everyone turned to watch him walk in. Laman and Lemuel came running, as did Shedrar, Hidai and Yavin, and Joab also approached, but only at a fast walk. Nephi could see the shocked look on his oldest brother-in-law's face, while the looks on Laman, Lemuel and the other men were of anger and confusion.

"I thought you said you could tie a knot!" yelled Shedrar at Lemuel.

"I did," retorted Lemuel. "I do not know how he could be free."

"Brothers, blame not Lemuel. I prayed unto the Lord, and he has loosed me. I tried Lemuel's knots with all of my strength and could not break free. Let this be a sign to you that what I have spoken is the truth."

"But how did you—" Joab started to speak but was cut off.

"Stop talking and get him," growled Laman, and he began to circle Nephi.

All of a sudden, between them, came running the youthful form of a young woman. Nephi looked and beheld Rachel. She started screaming, whirling to face her brothers and Nephi's brothers. "Leave him alone! He has done nothing but good for us—all of us! Nephi is our friend, and you are only jealous. Please!" In her frustration and anger, she began openly to weep, and a second female form came swiftly from the side to put her arm around her. This was Ra'ya, wife of Ishmael.

"My sons, please do not longer be the fools. You know how tightly you have bound Nephi's hands and feet, even against the pleas of Sam and Lotan and of the girls. And yet now he stands before you—freed. Is this not sign enough? How long can you blind yourselves to the truth that Nephi is a man of God? My sons, how long?"

Nephi's gaze shifted to Joab, and as it did he saw a light come over his eldest brother-in-law, and Joab turned suddenly to Shedrar, to Laman and Lemuel.

"My mother speaks the truth. I went along with what you wanted to do, because you were so angry, and for a little while your words seemed to have the strength of reason. And Nephi grabbed the arm of my wife, and I was angry. I am sorry for that now." Joab looked over apologetically at Nephi. "My sister is wrong—wrong not to have listened to Nephi when he wanted to talk. He tried to put hands on Jephthah, to heal him, and it was Zipporah who denied him.

"Has Nephi done things without our approval? Yes! He offered to save the six Bedouin, but this was not a gamble. He knew our daughter and two of our men would not be killed, and he knew that our women would not be taken. He *knew!* For the Lord was with him, as the Lord has always been if we would all but see it.

"And you, Laman, Lemuel and Shedrar—you should be most exceedingly ashamed. When your camels returned to our camp, it was Nephi who was sick with worry. It was Nephi who insisted on going out to look for you in the dark when the rest of us thought it prudent to wait until daylight.

"Nephi loves you, and if you cannot see this, then you are fools. And I do not perceive any of my brothers to be fools. It is the power of the devil which has blinded you—me. All of us. Let us cease this strife. The same man who can pray for his cords to be loosed, which all of us saw were tied tightly, and they are loosed—this same man doth receive revelations from the God of Israel. It is time for us to listen if we truly wish to be saved."

When Joab finished speaking, and his cheeks were wet with tears, there was a spirit that fell over the camp, a spirit of peace and love. It was a spirit that Laman and Lemuel, and even Shedrar, could not deny. The three of them, eyes full of tears, came in front of Nephi, and Laman took Nephi's wrist and bowed down, not able to look him in the eyes.

"It was the wine, little brother. Do not be angry with us. We had slept so little, and the wine was so powerful. We would have come back for you. We could not have left our brother in the wilderness to die. Please do not hate us. Please forgive us."

Lemuel echoed his brother's words, and this time even Shedrar, who seemed so perpetually angry with Nephi, dropped to his knees, and he shed tears—real tears—for what he had done.

Nephi smiled through his joyful tears. "My brothers, I do not hate you. I forgive you with all of my heart. Wine is a powerful thing, and I also know that there has been much tension in the camp. We have lost dear ones, not the least of which was your camel, Laman. And little Jephthah was a special spirit that all of us miss.

"I do not blame you for anything—not a single thing. But I think it would be meet if you would pray to the Lord for forgiveness as well. And if you pray with real intent you will feel a peace that most people can never know."

Nephi was not surprised when all three of them, along with Hidai, Gera, Yavin and Joab, took themselves out to pray away from camp. When they were gone, the spirit there only grew stronger, and Rachel and Ari'el came and hugged Nephi, as did even Sam and Lotan, Yona and Yael. Last, Ra'ya came before him.

"My son, please forgive me mine anger. I love my Ishmael so much that it grieves me to see him so ill. Like your brothers, and like mine own sons, I too have been blinded. You have done no wrong." She threw her arms around Nephi, and he stood and held her while she wept.

At last, when she stepped away from him and took his hands, she looked up into his kindly eyes. "Can I ask you to give my husband one more blessing, that he will be able to recover enough to at least ride upright with us on to the camp of your father and mother?"

"I will lay my hands on him, Mother Ra'ya. And I feel that the Lord will grant this."

And so the brothers returned to camp, smiling and talking in soft tones, and with the spirit of the Lord all around them they ate a quiet breakfast, finished loading the camels and, with the three horses trailing behind, started on their way to the Valley of Lemuel.

The arrival of the party of Ishmael in the Valley of Lemuel was a joyous one. For once, there was no contention among anyone, and rejoicing could be heard from afar. Ishmael and Ra'ya happily greeted their long-time friends Lehi and Sariah, and Sariah clasped her daughters to her, the daughters whom at one time she had believed to be lost to her forever. It was with sadness that the news of Jephthah's death was received by Lehi and Sariah, but the comfort of knowing he was with the Lord could not be weighed.

The joyous smile on Elnathan's face, and the real tears in his eyes when he saw his friend Nephi could never be measured in their value, and they embraced warmly before Elnathan stood back and put his big hand on the side of Nephi's head, cuffing him fondly.

No'ach, too, came running up and hugged Nephi, laughing heartily. "I feared you had been lost to the sands, or flown away like a flea—a *big* flea!"

Yona and Lotan saw these reunions through the eyes of strangers who were quickly taken into this family as if they had always been a part, and Lotan, overcome with the desire to pray, went off by himself and bowed his head to the Lord.

When Zoram came from the fields with Reuven and Ilai, where the barley harvest had been completed, and the wheat harvest was nearly done as well, his eyes were bright with emotion. Of course Nephi was the easiest person to spot because of his size, and Zoram's eyes rested upon him. Nephi felt himself being watched, and he stopped with Abraham's saddle in his hands and scanned around him, trying to find whose gaze called to him so strongly.

There stood his friend, his face filled with apprehension, and anticipation. Nephi smiled and gave his friend a nod, making

Zoram's face burst into a smile. It was all Zoram could do not to run to Nephi, and when he got to him he held out his hand so they could shake. "Welcome back, brother! My eyes are healed at the sight of you."

"And mine, Zoram. You have been much missed. By more than one of us."

The one-time servant of Laban searched Nephi's eyes. "Then... Yael—she has come?"

"She has come," replied Nephi, smiling broadly. "She is among us."

At that moment, Nephi stopped and looked to the far side of the camel pen, where Yona and Ginath were talking. There, on the far side of Yona, stood Yael. Her eyes were intent on her brother, and she seemed frozen in place.

"Go to her, my brother. I do not think she should have to wait."

Zoram, following the line of Nephi's gaze, turned and saw Yael, and then he ran, while Nephi followed him at a walk. With a heart that burst with joy, Nephi watched Zoram and Yael fall into each other's arms, and they held each other as if they never would let go. He caught up to them and stood by with Ginath and Yona, bowing his head happily as he waited. But it had not gone unnoticed to him before bowing his head the way that Ginath looked at his friend Zoram.

Zoram stepped away from Yael and took her face in his hands, staring at her with as much love as Nephi had ever beheld. "My sister is saved, saved by Nephi," was all his friend could say.

That night was a night of celebration, of prayer, and of sacrifice and burnt offerings unto the Lord. Until deep into the night the altar Lehi had built was kept busy, and the chosen people of the Lord prayed and laughed and sometimes wept for joy. Even Laman, Lemuel and Shedrar, who so often had seemed so angry, found themselves laughing and merry and friendly to all, even to Nephi. And Zipporah came to him in humility, bowed to him and asked for forgiveness. She had felt the Comforter come to her and promise her that her son was happy, wherever he was.

Ishmael, who had become well after Nephi placed his hands on his head and was allowed of the Lord to bless him with health and good traveling, told Lehi and Sariah of their journey, and of the many adventures they had shared. He recounted to everyone around the fire how Nephi had saved them all from sure destruction through his healing of the Bedouin, and he told of the sandstorm and of the wild beasts which they had encountered. Lehi sadly received the news of Naomi's demise, but the details of the story must wait, for Laman could not bring himself yet to tell all that had happened on that fateful and tragic evening.

Wine was passed around the circle, and it was partaken of in moderation and was good. In the valley of Lemuel, near the mouth of the softly gurgling River Laman, there was peace and love unsurpassed.

Chapter Seven

Lehi's Dream

There ensued an extended period of great harmony in the camp, marred only by the heat of the sun and the scouring winds that would rattle down through the gap of the sheer mountain walls that framed the valley. During this time, much celebration and joy continued, and prayer was common, not only by Lehi the prophet, but by his son Nephi, who had been chosen of the Lord to serve below him, and by many others in the camp, even those who did not fully understand the ways of the Lord. Elnathan was one who strove through his own prayers to understand, to learn the wisdom of Lehi and Nephi, and perhaps most of all to be forgiven for his past.

Sometime after the reunion, three smaller camps had grown out of the one, and Lehi and Sariah's contingent contained only Zoram, Lotan and their sons, with Elnathan and his friends in a second camp and all of the people of Ishmael in the largest camp, each separated by a hundred feet or so from the next.

In this time of separation, Lehi had a dream.

The dream was so powerful that the prophet awoke in the night and sat up, wondering for a time if it had been only a dream. But the Spirit of the Lord remained so strong in his heart, and so strongly burned his soul within him, that he knew this had been more than a dream. It was a vision, a message from God.

Creeping from his bed, Lehi lit an oil lamp and with a reed pen and some of their precious ink, which they made themselves out of soot, water, and gum Arabic, to make it stick, wrote on scrolls of parchment the details of his dream. Early the next evening, he gathered his family together to hear the things which the Lord had shown him.

"Because of my dream," said Lehi to his family, "I have reason to rejoice in the Lord because of Nephi and also of Sam. For I have reason to believe that they, and also many of their seed, will be saved.

"But I have also reason to fear exceedingly, and this for you, Laman and Lemuel, because of other things which I was shown in this vision. For these thoughts I mourn, because I love you both dearly and would not lose you if the choice be mine."

Lehi went on to recount his dream.

He witnessed a dark and dreary wilderness. And there he saw a man, and he was dressed in a white robe, and he came and stood before him. And he spoke to him and bade him follow.

As Lehi followed him into the wastelands, the man in the white robe was no longer to be seen. And after Lehi had traveled for many hours in darkness he began to pray unto the Lord to have mercy on him, for he felt hopelessly lost and abandoned.

When he had prayed, he opened his eyes and beheld a large and spacious field. In the field he saw a tree on which grew beautiful fruit which shone even from afar. He went to the fruit and ate of it and thought it was the sweetest he had ever tasted, sweeter than anything he had ever had before, even honey. In appearance, it was white, whiter also than anything he had ever seen.

Eating of the fruit filled Lehi with great joy, a joy he could hardly fathom or explain but which he knew was of the Lord. He was immediately desirous that his family should eat of the fruit as well. He cast his eyes round about, hoping to see his family, and beheld a river flowing with water. It ran along, flowing past the very tree from which he was partaking fruit.

He began to look up the river to see where it came from, and found that the head was only a little way off. There at the head stood Sariah, Sam and Nephi, and they were looking around as if they did not know where they should go.

Lehi beckoned to them and called out for them to come unto him and partake of this delicious fruit. To his joy, they came and also ate of the fruit, and he also wanted Laman and Lemuel to partake of it, so he looked for them at the head of the river. To his surprise, they stood there as well, but when he called to them and beckoned them near they would not come and eat the fruit in which the rest of his family found so much joy. He called and called to them, and both of them heard him, yet they turned and looked away, pretending not to hear.

As Lehi turned away from Laman and Lemuel, he noticed a rod of iron, and it extended along the bank of the river and led right up to the tree by which he stood. And paralleling the rod of iron was a strait and narrow path, also leading to the tree.

"This path," said Lehi, "led past the tree and to the fountain of the river, then to the large and spacious field, which began to seem to me as a world. And I saw numberless concourses of people, many of whom were pressing forward, that they might obtain the path which led unto the tree by which I stood."

He went on to say that the people came to the path and started down it toward the tree. But then there arose a mist of darkness, the same as the mists of darkness formed of dust and sand and the unexpected, extreme humidity often found in much of the Arabian desert, only this was greater than any he had ever beheld before, in all of his many travels. The darkness caused all of those who had started down the path to lose their way and wander off to become lost.

Then he saw others on the path, and these caught hold of the rod of iron. They pressed forward, able to come through the mists of darkness because they clung for all they were worth to the rod of iron. These people were able to make it to the beautiful tree, and they ate of its marvelous fruit, as Lehi and the others had done.

However, immediately upon eating of the fruit, these people began to look about as if they were ashamed. Lehi, wondering at this sudden shame in the eyes of these people, began to cast his eyes about, and on the other side of the river he noticed a great and spacious building that seemed to be floating in the very air, high above the earth. It was a kind of building which Lehi had never seen, and almost as if through its walls he could see that it was filled with people, both old and young, male and female, and their manner of dress was exceedingly fine. They seemed to be mocking and pointing their fingers towards the people who had come to the tree and were partaking of the fruit.

The people who had eaten of the fruit, who had begun to look ashamed, now allowed this shame to make them go from the tree, and they got onto many forbidden, dark paths and were lost, the same as the others before them who had never found the rod of iron.

After this, there came forth many more people to the tree, and when they reached it they fell down and ate of the white fruit. But many more people also felt their way toward the building hanging there in the air. Many of those were drowned trying to cross the fountain of the river, and many others were lost traveling on strange roads in the mists of darkness.

A great number of people ended up reaching the building, and then, like those who were already there, they began pointing at Lehi and his family in scorn, making fun of them for what they were doing. Lehi was happy to tell his family that in his dream they did not heed these mockers, yet he was sad to admit that Laman and Lemuel never did come to them and partake of the beautiful fruit of the tree.

When Lehi spoke these words, he stopped and looked around at his family, who gazed at him, enthralled. Even Laman watched him, and of them all only Lemuel could not meet his eyes except briefly. He walked over to Laman and Lemuel, who sat together, and he knelt before them on one knee.

"My sons, I know not with completeness what my dream signifies. I only know that I am very afraid. I am afraid for you, who have been such a joy to me and to your mother in your childhood days. I am so afraid for you that I sometimes wake in the night with shaking, and with tears lying on my cheeks, for I am frightened of what our future holds. There is so much good in both of you. So much good."

He reached up and took them each by a hand. "And we love you dearly, as only one who has children of their own could ever fathom. It is because of this love that I have so much fear that you should be cast off from the presence of the Lord. I believe you are good men, my sons, and you know what is right and what it takes to go back to live with the Lord after the sorrows of this world are over. So I am asking you with all that is in me that no matter what the future holds you do all that you can to hearken to the words of the Lord, that he will always be merciful to you."

Lehi went on preaching and prophesying to them, perhaps for a longer time than he should have, considering how Laman and Lemuel began to fidget. Having themselves singled out by their father in front of their younger brothers could not have been good for their emotional states, nor could they feel good about being chastised in front of their mother, for that was how this meeting seemed to come across to them.

Yet in truth most of what Lehi spoke was to all of his family, not simply to Laman and Lemuel, and these prophecies were something which the two oldest sons would have done well to listen to, for they spoke of the very truths that would save all mankind from destruction, in this life and in the life of spirits after the end of the world.

Lehi spoke of the coming of a prophet whom God would raise up among the Jews six hundred years from the time of their departure from Jerusalem. He would be a Messiah, or in other words a Savior of the world. And there should come before him another prophet, one who would baptize in Bethabara, and who would in due time baptize the Messiah himself.

Then he spake of how the Jews would harden their hearts and dwindle in unbelief, and in their hatred and in their blindness they would slay the very Messiah, who by his own power would rise again from the dead and make himself known, by the Holy Ghost, unto the Gentiles. In time, the house of Israel, likened unto an olive tree, would be broken off as branches, to be scattered upon all the face of the earth.

And Lehi told his family that they were a part of this scattering, and this was the reason that they were commanded to go now to the new land of promise, a land they knew not at this time. Then, at some far time, all of the house of Israel and even the Gentiles would come to a knowledge of the truth, and of the true Messiah, their Lord and their Redeemer.

When finally Lehi ceased to speak to them, Laman and Lemuel asked to be excused, and they left camp, headed up the valley away from the sea, and were not seen again for some time.

Laman and Lemuel walked far up the valley, leaving behind the kindly, beautiful oasis that had become their home. The country was dry, and all that had been green was now brown, and in many places there was no sign that grass had ever waved, for the goats, the sheep and camels had grazed it down to nothing.

The sheep and goats were bad in particular, which was why in some circles they were detested, because they would eat the grass right down to the very roots, along with anything else that happened into their way that even resembled food. Sometimes it did not even have to resemble food, but simply something to put in their mouths! And then their sharp hooves would slice the grass roots and kill them so they could not return.

The brothers did not speak for a mile or more, as both of them brooded over the harsh and frightening words their father had said.

Many times, Laman thought to speak, in his anger, then decided against it and continued walking, trying to get hold of his temper so as not to look the fool. When they were far from the oasis, and it was no longer even in sight, he finally reached down and picked up a stone, flinging it as far out across the sand as he could. An ugly, long-eared rabbit had been seated in the shade of a bush, and it darted out in serpentine fashion across the desert flat, raising a zigzag cloud of dust in its wake.

When Laman spoke, it was not of the coming of a Messiah, or of the redeeming of the house of Israel. It seemed he had missed Lehi's most important message. "Well, brother, how did you enjoy that?"

Lemuel looked up, cringing. Even though he and Laman were best friends, he did not like it when his brother went on a rampage, and he had feared this tempest ever since they walked out of camp. "What can I say?"

"Say? What can you say? Say that you are angry with our father for chastising us in front of his most perfect son, his angel boy prophet who can do no wrong! What makes Nephi special, Lemuel? You and I went to Jerusalem to help bring back the plates of brass. We went once more to fetch Ishmael and his family and returned to camp happy to see Father and Mother.

"We have helped with the last of the wheat harvest, we have helped with the threshing and the winnowing. We have done all that was asked of us. We have even prayed, with just as much faith as anyone else. So why this? Why now? Have we done something wrong? A dream! Lemuel, can you imagine that? Father has a dream, and because of this now in his sight we are evil. We are going to follow the devil and destroy all who are about us. *Because of a dream!*

"Well, I will tell you whom I would like to destroy: Nephi! When will the curse of him ever leave us? Tell me that! This torment goes on and on, and even when there is no reason for it, and we have said not so much as a cross word, we are berated in front of the perfect child, the baby prophet. I grow very tired of this. I would that we had never left Jerusalem, that we had remained in the land of our inheritance. We are fools to be out here, treated as camels, or asses, or worse!"

"I know," agreed Lemuel. "I do not like it either. Maybe one day Nephi will get killed by a lion—could we be so lucky?"

Laman scoffed. "Lemuel, that little boy who believes himself so far above us, his rightful leaders, is blessed—blessed of the devil. I truly think the devil controls him and is using him as a tool to deceive everyone around him, especially our father. No, he will not die—not unless a brave enough man takes it upon himself and strives against the very devil we all fear. Until that day, our little brother will plague us—mark my words."

As Laman and Lemuel left to walk up the valley, Nephi excused himself to go out and care for the animals. Sam jumped up and ran after him, and together they walked from camel to camel and even looked to the goats and the sheep, whose numbers by now had dwindled from using them as a food source, and occasionally for sacrifices to God. They sought now for any that were sick or which might have stones lodged in their feet.

Sam kept his silence as long as he could before he began to ask Nephi what he thought of this prophecy of a Messiah, and of their imminent journey to the land of promise.

Nephi, whose own mind had been full with thoughts of his father's speech, turned to Sam, his face aglow. "We are on the brink of one of the greatest and most important adventures ever known to man, Sam! This I know of a surety. I cannot even begin to tell you of the joy that fills my heart. I think it will take a long time, perhaps even days, before I can speak of these things, for great emotions engulf my soul.

"Sam, think of it—a promised land, perhaps a new world of which we do not even know. We will pray hard and be kind to Laman and Lemuel, and to the sons of Ishmael, and I believe their hearts will be softened, and they will desire to come with us to this new land. I will be forever glad that we were able to keep our brothers from returning to Jerusalem, where they would have been destroyed, for they will be important in our future, as we cannot even now know. I feel this all in my heart."

Sam was beaming. "You are strong, my brother. When you speak I feel the power of God through you, even when you speak of simple things. We will always be together, until death draws us apart. And one day you will lead this family in righteousness, after the passing of our father. The spirit hath spoken this to me."

Chapter Eight

Nephi's Vision

For a day, Nephi pondered the vision of his father, and the other prophecies of which he had spoken. So badly did he want to see these things for himself, and to know what the dream signified. He also desired to have it confirmed to him that his feelings about Laman and Lemuel were right, that he could love them and show them enough kindness and respect that they would repent and learn to follow the ways of the Lord and they would be great men in their time, and great leaders of men.

During this time, as he pondered, he wandered alone in the valley, and there late in the evening his friend Elnathan found him, tarrying by one of the large monoliths, this one all of two hundred feet high and perhaps a hundred yards around.

"And how is my young brother Nephi today?" asked the one-time manhunter and prince of Jerusalem. His eyes were filled with a love and respect for Nephi that no other could surpass.

"I am well, Elnathan. And ever happy to behold your face before me."

Elnathan smiled and laid a heavy hand on Nephi's shoulder. As powerful and as big of frame as Nephi had grown, the size of his hands, his arms, his torso would never match the sheer bulk of Elnathan.

"What troubles your heart this eve?"

"It is not so much troubled as wondering. My father spoke to our family of a vision, and he foretold of many things to come, things of which I would speak to you one day very soon. Yet I find this deep desire within me to know these things of myself, to see the same things which my father hath seen, and also to know their meaning."

"The words of your father did not suffice?"

"Nay, for he did not understand all of the things of his dream himself. It spake of strange things, of a white tree with beautiful white fruit that was delicious to taste, of people who would partake of it while others would not. Many strange things such as this—and it singled out Laman and Lemuel, for they were of those who would not partake."

Elnathan stopped now, and Nephi with him. The camp was a long ways away, hidden by the forest of palm trees. Elnathan again raised his arm and let his hand rest on his friend's shoulder. Their eyes met, and in Elnathan's was this deep green light that shone, a light that had appeared and grown over the time Nephi had known his friend.

"I have learned many things here in this valley, Nephi, things that I am certain you know already. But sometimes everyone forgets. One of the things I have learned, and it has helped me to see things I would never have dreamed possible, is to fast with my prayer.

"While you were gone, I fasted and prayed before the barley harvest began, for I wanted to know the things you know and to feel the spirit as you feel it, so that we can be as one in our hearts. Your father taught me this truth, and I would remember it to you. Go, fast and pray, and if you want I will go with you, to guard you from the beasts of the wild. Go up to the mountains and find what you are seeking."

And so Nephi did just as his wise friend bade him. That night he refused to eat supper, and very early the next morning, when the light was breaking gray and misty, he and Elnathan set out into the depths of the mountains, where the ibex and the oryx found safety among the peaks and the sleek yellow leopard lurked and sought its prey in the halls of shadow.

Of nourishment for himself, Elnathan brought an ample supply, and he brought water, dates and dried meat for the return journey, that Nephi might also regain his strength. When they had climbed ten or twelve miles into the mountains, far from the filth and commotion and the hordes of fleas that were growing in the camp, when they had chosen a clearing that nestled among the stones and the greenery that could be seen here that was no longer found below, Nephi, who had been without food now for some twenty-four hours, sat himself with legs crossed upon the ground.

Elnathan scaled up into the higher rocks to a vantage point where he could look down upon Nephi's station, a place where he could see any creeping or lurking thing that might approach and wish to do his friend harm. And here he remained, throughout that bitter cold night and throughout the heat of the following day.

And Nephi fasted, taking in no water and no morsel of food, only sitting still in his little nest with no robes and with nothing to cover his torso and pondering in his heart the things of his father's dream.

And in the second night, sometime well after dark and bone-piercing cold had descended, as Nephi was pondering, his body weak from hunger and thirst and from the cold, but his spirit grown stronger for the same reasons, he was caught away in the Spirit of the Lord.

He seemed to be up in a high mountain, one which he had never seen and where he had never set his foot. And the spirit said to him, "Behold, what desirest thou?"

And he said, speaking as if to a friend, that he wanted to see all of the things which his father had seen. And the spirit said, "Believest thou that thy father saw the tree of which he hath spoken?" When Nephi answered yes, that he believed all the words of his father, the spirit cried out with a loud voice, saying, "Hosanna to the Lord, the most high God, for he is God over all the earth, yea, even above all. And blessed art thou, Nephi, because thou believest in the Son of the most high God. Wherefore, thou shalt behold the things which thou hast desired."

The spirit told him that he should have a sign, that after he had witnessed the same white tree which his father had seen he should then see a man descending out of heaven, and after he had seen him he would bear record that it was the Son of God.

The spirit then told Nephi to look, and there stood the tree, every bit as white as Lehi had described, even whiter than the driven snow. The beauty was beyond all beauty Nephi had ever witnessed. Now, speaking as a man speaks to another, he told the spirit, when asked, that he desired to know the meaning of the tree. As he spoke, he knew that this spirit was the Spirit of the Lord.

Soon, the Spirit of the Lord disappeared, and he was nowhere to be seen. But there before Nephi was the great city of Jerusalem, and there were also other cities. Jerusalem was not the same city he had left, and only by the high ridge on which it stood and by the surroundings did he know it, for it was a much grander place, the outer walls much higher, the temple and the king's palace far more beautiful and glorious than any city which he had ever beheld and than the city to which he and his family had bid farewell.

And he beheld the city called Nazareth, and in this city he beheld a young maiden he perceived to be a virgin, who was exceedingly fair and white.

The heavens now opened, and an angel came down and stood in front of Nephi, and he asked, "Nephi, what beholdest thou?"

Nephi answered, "A virgin, most beautiful and fair above all other virgins."

The angel then asked if Nephi knew of what he termed the condescension of God, and Nephi answered that he did not know the meaning of all things, only that God loved his children. So the angel told him that the virgin he was looking at was the mother of the Son of God, who was coming to earth in flesh.

Nephi saw that the virgin, like he, was carried away in the spirit for a time, and when the angel told him to look he saw the virgin again, and in her arms she bore a child. The angel said solemnly, "Nephi, behold the Lamb of God, even the Son of the Eternal Father."

And even in his vision, Nephi had tears in his eyes, for the child was very beautiful and touched his soul in a way he did not then understand.

After a time, the angel asked, "Knowest thou the meaning of the tree which thy father saw?"

Nephi suddenly knew the answer, and he replied that it was the love of God and was the most desirable of all things. The angel confirmed this, and he showed Nephi a vision of the Son of God, now grown, going forth among the children of men, and many of these fell down at his feet to worship him.

Spread throughout these visions, Nephi continued to learn the things of his father's dream. He learned that the rod of iron was meant to signify the word of God, which led to the fountain of living waters or to the tree of life. The tree of life was meant as

the love of God, and the fountain and the river of water were re-
vealed to Nephi as being of filthy water, something which Lehi
had not seen because he had been caught up in so many other
things at once.

And the filthy waters represented an awful gulf which separated the wicked from the tree of life and also from the saints of
God. It was the hell which was prepared for the wicked. And the
mists of darkness were the temptations of the devil, which
blindeth the eyes and harden the hearts of the children of men,
and leadeth them away into broad roads, that they perish and are
lost.

The wonderful vision continued, and Nephi beheld again the
Redeemer of the world, the Son of God, and also the prophet who
would come before him. The Lamb of God was baptized of this
prophet, and after he was baptized Nephi beheld the heavens
open, and the Holy Ghost came down and lit upon him in the form
of a dove.

The Redeemer then went forth administering unto the people
in great glory, and the multitudes gathered together to hear him,
but then cast him out from among them. There were also twelve
others following him, and all of them were then carried away in
the spirit, and he saw them no longer.

He saw the Lamb of God healing those who were sick and
afflicted, and from others who were possessed of devils and unclean spirits he did exorcise these spirits and devils. He also did
raise people from the dead. Then, even after all the righteous
deeds he had done, the Lamb of God was taken by the people,
judged of the world, and then, to Nephi's horror, he was lifted up
upon a wooden cross and slain, dying for the sins of the world.

Then, after the Lamb was slain, the multitudes of the earth
continued in their evil ways, gathering together to fight against
the apostles, for thus were the twelve called by the angel of the

Lord. This multitude gathered together in a large building, and this was like the large and spacious building which Lehi had beheld in his dream.

The angel told him that this was the world and the wisdom and the pride thereof, the house of Israel which had gathered together to fight against the twelve apostles. And soon the building fell, and the fall thereof was exceedingly great, and the angel said to Nephi, "Thus shall be the destruction of all nations, kindreds, tongues and people that shall fight against the twelve apostles of the Lamb."

There was a moment when Nephi seemed alone, and then as he pondered, the angel began to reveal unto him things that were even more immediate to him, for he showed unto him his descendants and the descendants of his brothers, and he saw the land of promise, and it was beautiful above all other lands Nephi had ever witnessed. He beheld multitudes of people, in number as the sands of the sea, and they were gathered together to battle one against another. And he continued to foresee wars and great slaughters among his people.

He observed the passing of many generations, all in war and contention, and he saw many cities, so many that he did not try to count them. Soon, he observed a mist of darkness upon the land of promise, and there came lightning and thunder and earthquakes and all manner of tumultuous noises. The earth and the rocks broke up, and mountains fell to pieces, and the plains also shattered. Many cities sank into the sea, and many burned with awesome fire, and many others tumbled down in the midst of the earthquakes.

After he had watched all these horrible things, the vapor of darkness lifted and passed from off the face of the earth, and there were multitudes of people who had survived the great destruction of the world. The heavens opened then, and the Lamb of God descended out of heaven and came down to show himself unto the people of the promised land. The Holy Ghost came and fell upon twelve others who were not the apostles of the Lamb in the Old World, and they were ordained of God.

The angel told Nephi that these were twelve apostles, like unto the other twelve, who would administer unto his descendants in the New World. And the first twelve would judge the twelve tribes of Israel, and the twelve new apostles would judge Nephi's seed, for they were righteous forever, because of their faith in the Lamb of God.

Nephi then saw and was comforted by three generations who passed away in righteousness, and also many of the fourth generation who also remained righteous until the end. Then it came to pass that he saw the multitudes of the earth, the seed of Nephi and also of his brothers. Nephi was sad to see that once more the two factions were gathered together to do battle.

The seed of his brethren contended against his seed, and because of the pride of his seed and the temptations of the devil, the descendants of his brethren overpowered his own. And then the descendants of his brethren went forth in multitudes upon the face of the land, and even they gathered together in multitudes to war one against another. In this way, many generations did pass.

Again there was a time of silence, and then the angel began to show Nephi many things that were to come to pass in the far away future, of a Gentile who sailed across the great waters to discover the descendants of his brothers, and of others who escaped captivity and also came to the shores of the promised land.

There were many more wars, and the seed of Nephi's brethren were smitten by the Gentiles, and the Gentiles did prosper and obtain the land for their inheritance. These Gentiles were white of skin as Nephi's people had been before they were slain.

And then the angel spoke of two books, one which came from the Jews and had been stripped of many plain and precious truths, and another, a book that rose out of the seed of Nephi, that kept all of those plain and precious things but which also attested to the truth of the first book and to the mercy of the Lamb of God.

And lastly, when Nephi felt utterly exhausted of spirit, the angel spoke unto him and told him that there would be two churches, the one being the church of the Lamb of God, and the other being the church of the devil. And the members of the church of the Lamb of God in numbers were few, and the other church, which was referred to as the whore of all the earth, had dominion over all the earth, among all nations, kindreds, tongues and people. Yet even so, the church of God, in its small numbers, was also in all the face of the earth.

And the angel showed unto Nephi a man dressed in a white robe, and he was one of the twelve apostles of the Lamb. And his name was John. And this man would write of the contentions between the abominable church and the church of the Lamb, and he would write of the end of the world, and his writings would be contained in the book which came from the Jews.

And Nephi saw many more things which he was forbidden to speak of or write, and then, in the blackest depths of the darkness of night, he awoke. He was lying on the ground, cold and shivering, his face and even his hair wet with many tears, and looking up at a sky filled with crystalline stars.

Like a dead man, Nephi lay staring at the sky, frozen in place, unable to move as much as a finger. His eyes were blurred, and that made the stars shimmer as reflections in a vast body of water. He had never felt more exhausted, more physically, mentally and emotionally spent—and spiritually as well.

He tried to rise, but his head began to reel, nausea swept over him, and then he felt himself slipping into total blackness, as if he were being drawn down into that endless gulf, that filthy river of water, the depths of hell.

And then he knew no more.

Chapter Nine

Translating the Dream

"Nephi. Nephi. Wake up, brother. Nephi!"

It was a dream. Nephi tried to move his head. He tried to open his eyes. Someone was calling to him, a soothing voice, a voice of one he loved. Who was this? It was so far away, so unreachable. He wanted to call back to them, to ask where they were. He wanted to reach out a hand, to beg for help, but there was none.

"Nephi, open your eyes. You need to move. It is cold here."

Cold? Yes, it was cold. So very cold. He seemed to be shaking. There was a wind, and it was stroking his hair on his forehead, and it tickled, but he could not move it, could not even raise a finger, to say nothing of his hand.

He felt a touch on his forehead. It was a hand, a heavy hand, and it was warm. It brushed away the hair, and then it began to vigorously massage his shoulders and arms, and like a river caked with mud he felt his blood begin to course in his veins, and his skin tingled. Fighting, fighting, he struggled to open his eyelids, and finally they flickered, and there was a stab of light. He shut them again, only for a moment, and then he felt his fingers moving.

He tried his eyes again, and this time they opened, and the light was not so fierce as he had thought, only a dull sheen like moonlight on polished iron. Someone was bent over him, a large head, he thought, but too blurred to make out. The person smiled. He could see the flash of teeth, and he could see a black beard.

"You have had a long night, my friend."

He recognized the voice now. His friend Elnathan, prince of Jerusalem, hunter of men such as Lehi and his sons. Reformed man of God and mighty man of valor.

Nephi tried to smile as he saw Elnathan's big, shaggy head coming into focus. He was able to raise his hand, and Elnathan's huge paw closed over it.

"How fare ye?" asked Elnathan.

"I am alive—I think."

Elnathan gave a hearty laugh. "You are alive, yes. But as cold as a fish. I should make you a fire. Have you seen anything of what you came to see?"

The many things that Nephi had witnessed in the spirit came washing back through his mind, piece by piece, scene by scene. He saw the blood, the carnage, the seed of his brothers fighting against his own seed and the seed of Sam. He saw the fall of his people. He saw the murder of the Lamb of God, and the mighty destruction that befell the world when the Lamb was dead.

He saw mists of darkness, and great walls of flame and smoke, and beautiful, magnificent buildings that crumbled into the sea. He saw mountains of rock rent in twain, and plains broken and heaved and ablaze with fire. And then he saw the perfect Lamb descending from the heavens, shining brilliant with light as bright as the sun.

His eyes filled with the tears of the memories, and he was silent, and he closed his eyes.

And he heard Elnathan's quiet voice above him, filled with awe and reverence. "Yes, you have seen it, my friend. I fear perhaps you have seen too much for you to stand."

Nephi wept, and but for that sound and the gargle of a distant raven there was deathly silence in the mountain and all of Nephi's universe, and all of the spirits of the men and women of the world gone by seemed hushed and aghast at the shadows of things in the world to come.

When next Nephi was aware of anything it was warmth, and a man singing in a gruff voice, but not a bad voice. He could smell woodsmoke and hear a crackling and a hissing noise now and then, and he turned his head to gaze at the softly fluttering flames of the fire, bright against the purple rocks.

The sky was lighter now, almost as the gray of a turtle dove, and Nephi rolled onto his side and put out his arm shakily. He raised up on his hand and sat sideways, looking into the fire. Suddenly, he looked up and Elnathan was studying his face, and the big man smiled.

"Dates, my friend?"

Nephi smiled, struggling to get into a more comfortable position, sitting cross-legged in front of the merry fire his friend was nursing. "Dates sound good. Unless you have only the dung of a camel, for I think I could eat that if it were it were the only thing before me."

Elnathan laughed. "You have gone long without food. Sorry, but I have just finished off the last of the camel dung. You will have to settle for dates." He held out a large handful of dried dates, and Nephi took them and gingerly ate a couple, chewing slowly. "You saw what you came for," Elnathan stated, and his voice was deep and grave.

Nephi nodded. "I saw much, my friend. I saw more than I would have asked for—more than any man should ever wish to see. More than I would want anyone I loved to have to endure."

"Do I ever want to know? Do you think me strong enough?"

Nephi studied his friend. "You more than most. And in time I will ask you to pray with me and then to hear it. But now I have no strength to speak of it. Elnathan, I have seen the murder of the Son of God, and the destruction and the bitter end of all the world."

When Nephi had enough strength, and when the sun had at last boiled upward into the steely heaven, he and Elnathan scattered the ashes of the little fire and walked away out of the mountain, leaving it to the ravens and the circling buzzards and the beasts that roamed the vast wild land.

They made a path straightway to Lehi's tent, for Nephi wanted to tell his father what had happened. But as they approached it Nephi saw Laman and Lemuel standing at the front, and when he came closer, walking softly, he could hear their voices. Even two days after Lehi spoke to them, it surprised him to hear that they were disputing over the things Lehi had told them, of his dreams and of the other prophecies.

Nephi's first reaction was to run to them, to try to help them understand. He would have to, because they were so hard of heart that they would not go to the Lord in prayer as they should. This grieved Nephi greatly, for having seen the destruction of his people he knew all these terrible things should come to pass, and he wished with all his heart he could save his brothers from this. But as he moved toward the tent, hoping to speak to them, his knees suddenly gave way, and he found himself seated on the ground, eased there by Elnathan, who had seen him weakening and had caught him.

Feeling the tears well up in him again, Nephi lowered his head and gritted his teeth. He sat there in silence with Elnathan for many minutes, listening to the angry discussion of Laman and Lemuel, wishing somehow they could become more like Sam, faithful, spiritual Sam. It was a long time before he felt the strength to rise, and without a word Elnathan helped him up. He then turned to his friend and said quietly, "Let me go to them and speak alone, so they will not think they are being chastised again in front of others."

"You are certain this is what you want to do?"

"I am certain. And thank you for your help on the mountain. Without you there I do not know what might have become of me."

"My love for you is endless, Nephi. I would not have let you go alone."

After Elnathan had gone quietly away, Nephi stepped around the tent and said, "Good morning, brothers."

The two of them whirled on him, eyeing him suspiciously. "Morning," replied Laman.

"I hear that you are troubled by what Father spoke to us. What makes you dispute these things?"

"Did he send you here?" asked Laman.

"Father? No. *I* came to see *him*. I have come from off the mountain."

"We were told you went up there to pray," said Laman, nodding. "You do not look well." A concerned look crossed his face, but he appeared to force it away. "Did you take our wine with you?"

Lemuel laughed at this, but Laman only smirked at his brother, then looked back at Nephi.

"I was praying to see the vision, to see all of the things that our father saw," said Nephi. "What is troubling you?"

"The things Father said to us seem very hard to understand, and we wonder why it could not simply have been a dream. I myself have had many dreams that made no sense. Why does everything to our father have to be a vision?" asked Laman.

"I do not know that everything does, brother. But this was, for I fasted long and prayed and have witnessed the same things while

I was on the mountain. And many more, enough to grieve the heart of the mightiest man."

"Then what meaneth Father about the natural branches of the olive tree, and what of the Gentiles?" asked Lemuel.

"Have ye inquired of the Lord in prayer?"

Laman scoffed. "Come, Nephi! The Lord has not chosen us, as he has you and our father. We have prayed before, yet he maketh no such things known unto us."

"Brothers, I do not want to be harsh, but the Spirit of the Lord constrains me to say things that will to you seem hard. How is it that you do not keep the commandments of the Lord, especially when you have seen so many great and wonderful miracles? Why do you put yourself in danger of perishing, by the hardening of your hearts?

"Remember what the Lord hath said: If ye will not harden your hearts to him, and if you will ask in faith, believing that ye shall receive, with diligence in keeping the commandments, surely all things will be made known unto you.

"But to set your minds at ease as to these things you ask me about, the house of Israel was compared unto an olive tree, and are we not broken off from the house of Israel, and a branch of this olive tree, and are we not a part of the house of Israel?"

Nephi went on to speak of the Gentiles, of how they played into the plan of the Lord, and he spoke of the prophecies of Isaiah, and of the restoration of the Jews in the latter days. And to Nephi's own surprise, as he continued to speak, going on for some fifteen minutes, a light came into Laman and Lemuel's eyes, and they truly seemed to understand, when Nephi put Lehi's dream into plain language. There were no harsh words from Laman and Lemuel, as Nephi had expected, and they appeared humbled before the Lord.

They all ended up taking seats in front of the tent, while everyone else was out away from camp, and Laman and Lemuel continued pressing Nephi with questions, about the meaning of the white tree, the fruit, the iron rod, and the strait and narrow path. Nephi, with much gladness, told them the meaning of all these things, and it was as if he were teaching young students who were eager to learn. His heart was full to overflowing as he saw the wonder in their faces, and his soul was filled with burning hope.

In answering his brothers' questions, Nephi spoke of hell, and of how they would be judged of their works which were done by the temporal body in their days of probation. He talked of how if they should die in their wickedness they must be cast off, and they must be brought to stand before God to be judged of their works, and how if their works were filthy they could not dwell in the kingdom of God.

And Nephi said to them boldly, "Behold, I say unto you, the kingdom of God is not filthy, and there cannot any unclean thing enter into it. Wherefore there must needs be a place of filthiness prepared for that which is filthy. And that place is the awful hell of which I have spoken, and the devil is he who made it. The final state of the souls of men will be to live either in this hell, if their deeds have been filthy, or to live in the kingdom of God, if they have done good."

For a long time, Laman and Lemuel sat staring at the ground, contemplating the words of their younger brother. He was happy that Shedrar was not here, for it seemed that, for the first time in many days they were actually listening to him, and there was no one to stir them up to unreasonable anger.

At last, Laman looked up and met Nephi's eyes, searching them. "Brother, you have declared hard things to us. It is almost too much to take."

"I spoke hard things against the wicked, Laman. Hard things, but true things. But I have also said the righteous will be lifted up at the last day. The guilty hear the truth and take it to be hard, because it cuts them to the core. If you two will become righteous and hearken to the truth, to the things you have been taught from your youth, and walk uprightly before God, then you would not murmur because of these hard things, because they would not pertain unto you.

"I have seen hard, horrible things in my vision on the mountain, and in time I will have the strength to tell it all. That time comes quickly, but before then, I beg you to keep the commandments of the Lord with all your diligence, because as Father said there are very hard things that await you if you do not, and I do not want to lose two brothers that I love with all my heart."

Laman stood up and walked to Nephi, and for a moment he stood looking down at him before Nephi finally got up, meeting the confused look in his older brother's eyes.

"Nephi, we have done hard things to you, and spoken many words of hurt. We even bound you with cords and planned to leave you in the wilderness to be devoured by wild animals. Why do you always say you love us? Why do you care what happens to us? More than anything else, I cannot understand this."

Nephi smiled and put a hand on his brother's shoulder. "Since I was a very young boy you have been a hero to me, Laman. You are my brother, he in whose footsteps I always desired to follow. I could never not love you."

A sudden flood of tears filled Laman's eyes, and he stepped forward and clasped Nephi in his arms, laughing. Nephi felt Lemuel pat him on the arm, and he looked at his second oldest brother with tears in his eyes. Lemuel was smiling.

"Thank you for the faith you keep in us, little brother," said Lemuel. "We have not been good to live with, and we will do better. I promise you that."

But Laman could not speak at all, and as he smiled at his brother, all he could do was raise a hand to put it alongside Nephi's cheek and to smile up at him through his tears.

Chapter Ten

A Wedding Feast

There was peace in the Valley of Lemuel. Peace, and there was love. It was customary among Jewish families that the younger daughters should not marry until the oldest found her husband. And while this custom had technically been fulfilled because Ginath had already been married to Yerach and had since become widowed, Ishmael did not feel it was meet that his younger daughters should marry the sons of Nephi while Ginath was a widow and there were other eligible bachelors in the camp.

Fortunately, the Lord had forged a way for Ginath not only to have a husband, but to find love as well, for she and Zoram had been naturally attracted to each other from the first time they met. Zoram did not hide his feelings long, and he felt peace from his long-lost Eden when he went to Ishmael and asked for Ginath's hand.

In Jewish society, the bridegroom, known as the *hatan,* or more often his father or some other go-between, would confront the prospective bride's father and offer a *mohar,* which might be gold or silver, fine linens or something else of value. In some cases it might be a service.

In Zoram's case, since he had nothing of great value to offer, it was service he chose to present. Seeing that Ishmael did not appear to be very healthy, Zoram made the promise by his name and that of his father to always provide assistance to the family of Ishmael in any way that he could. Perceiving the younger man's good heart and the feelings he had for his daughter, and understanding that in this wilderness things simply were not how they would have been back in Jerusalem, this was accepted by Ishmael as Zoram's mohar, and the arrangements were made.

There were many marriage traditions that could not be kept under the circumstances, not only for Zoram but also for the sons of Lehi. For Lehi, it had long been understood that his sons would marry the daughters of Ishmael, and the gifts and the arrangements were mere technicality. After they had been offered, and the betrothal period began, it could in no way be expected to last for the one to two year time period that would have been customary for a marriage in Jerusalem.

This was a period when the groom-to-be spent his time preparing gifts, called the *mattan,* for his bride, and also adding a room onto the house of his father. Since none of this was feasible, and since in Lehi's camp these husbands and wives, as they were called from the time of the betrothal, were living in close proximity to each other, and thus not able to be out of contact during the betrothal period as was normally required by tradition, it was sensibly decided that the betrothal period should be severely shortened and the wedding day begin immediately.

To the delight of all in the camp, when the big day came, it was not just a celebration of five weddings, but of six, for on this day Yona the dove gave her hand to her beloved Lotan son of Merav.

The wedding celebration in the Valley of Lemuel was magnificent, and it was attended by more than just the families of Ishmael and Lehi, and Elnathan and his comrades. The sheikh Bahram learned of the weddings, and on the very morning of the celebration his entire tribe arrived bedecked in their finest clothing.

The sheikh himself wore, to hold his shroud in place, a headband of gold filigree that was lined with the very finest gems. He wore large rings on his fingers, one of them looking much like the one he had gifted to Nephi, and a necklace which hung down to the middle of his chest, and in its center gleamed a huge red piece of polished coral.

By Jewish custom, it was generally required of wedding guests to be invited to the ceremony and to come dressed in a wedding garment of linen. But in the case of the sheikh and his Bedouin people, the Jews were honored to have them and would never have turned them away on this technicality. It was by far not the most honored of traditions broken that day.

Besides bringing gifts for those to be married, Bahram also brought a huge tent, bigger than the one Ishmael and his family had brought from Jerusalem originally, and decorated extravagantly with embroidered pictures of scarlet ibises and the hooved animals of the mountains, as well as a caravan of camels. He presented this to Ishmael and Ra'ya, bowing before them. "It is my gift to you for the one which I have burned," he said, and Ra'ya, crying, kissed the sheikh upon the cheek as he arose.

The Bedouin brought for the wedding feast four young camels, the pride of their tribe almost as much as their horses were. They made huge fires laid in pits in the ground and began one by one to slay the young camels, and as the fires died down to coals, they lay the camel carcasses, hair, hide and all, in the pit and began to roast them, and the aroma filled the air.

Neither Lehi nor Ishmael had the heart to tell the sheikh that in Jewish tradition the actual feast was not to begin until the bride and groom had been married for a full seven days. After all, as long as they were going to a new "promised land," why not start their own traditions as they went? But at much larger issue was the breaking of the Law of Moses, for in the book of Leviticus the Jews were specifically commanded not to eat the camel, because being of uncloven foot he was unclean unto them.

Even among the prophets of old, there were many instances in scripture of the laws being broken, among them many of the laws about the taking of wives and mistresses. With that in mind, and in light of the sheikh's utter generosity in offering such a precious gift, Lehi and Ishmael for a time both thought that perhaps this one time they might be allowed to partake of the meat of unclean beasts. After all, it was only a ceremonial impurity anyway, and it was stated in the book of Leviticus that by evening the state of uncleanness would end. However, that was before Nephi came to them.

The young man stood by his father and Ishmael for a time as they chatted. Out of deference to them, for some time he was silent, until Lehi finally turned to him. "My son, did you wish to speak?"

"Yes, Father. It is an important matter."

"What is it?"

"Father, have you seen that Bahram and his people are preparing young camel for our feast?"

Lehi cleared his throat, throwing Ishmael a quick glance. "Yes, we did. Ishmael and I have been speaking of this. We have decided that we will partake of the meat and ask for a blessing of forgiveness. Bahram has become our friend, and we would not want to offend him in his generous gift."

Nephi stood silent for a moment while trying to meet the forthright gazes of his two elders. "Something more, my son?" asked Lehi finally.

Nephi gave them a smile. "Father, I do not want to show any disrespect to you or to Father Ishmael. But..."

"You are a man, Nephi. Speak your mind."

Nephi took a deep breath. "Then, Father, I believe that we should not partake. If Bahram is truly our friend, he would not want us to offend our God. Should we not be more afraid of offending our Lord than of offending a man?"

There was a long moment of silence. Both Lehi and Ishmael stared at Nephi, then looked at each other. Finally, Ishmael began to laugh. "What is funny?" growled Lehi.

"This," said Ishmael, waving a hand across the three of them. "You. I. Your son. Lehi, my friend, he is right. It is safer to take the chance of offending a mere mortal than to offend the one who has given us everything we have."

Lehi suddenly looked defeated. He drew in a deep breath and clasped a hand on Ishmael's strong shoulder, leaving it lay there as he turned his eyes to his son. "I am stilled, Nephi. I feel the fool. You are right. Very right. The boy I used to teach has become a man and is teaching me." He nodded briskly. "I will go talk to him."

Nephi quickly shook his head. "No, Father. Please let me."

"You are sure?"

"I am."

"All right, then. Call me if you would like. I will remain right here."

With his straight bearing, Nephi walked directly to the place where Bahram was lounging in the shade of a palm tree, watching his sons prepare the carcasses of the young camels. The sheikh watched him walked up and started to rise, but Nephi stopped him.

"No, Master. Please. I beg you sit."

Bahram smiled. "Very well. Then please, my son. Sit."

Nephi sat down next to him. "What may I do for you?" asked Bahram.

"I see that you have brought much meat," Nephi said.

"Yes," said Bahram proudly. "The meat of the young camel is delicious and nourishing. It is the best we have—for you, my friends."

Nephi smiled. He felt a calming presence come over him. "My sheikh, it is a kind gift. Very thoughtful and very generous. It will not be overlooked."

The sheikh cocked his head, trying to read the something else that he could see behind Nephi's eyes. "And yet...?"

Nephi decided simply to barge on. This was not a time for meekness. "And yet, my good friend, we are not allowed to partake. Our laws tell us that we are not to partake of unclean animals—that is, animals that do not chew their cud, or animals without cloven hooves. This is a very strict law that was given to us at the time of our great prophet Moses."

Bahram glanced beyond Nephi, to the place where his sons were busy with their preparations. Finally, he looked back. "But my sons, they have gone to so much work. And you know that we do not kill these calves lightly. There are very precious to us. Just this once, Nephi, could you not forget your law?"

Nephi was still. There was a voice inside that begged him to please agree, to simply say yes and keep the peace. It would make an old man happy, an old man that he truly had come to think a lot of. But to compromise now, what would it mean in his future? Especially, what would Laman and Lemuel and the others think if they broke the law now? How would they, in the future, be able to look them in the eyes when asking them to obey the laws of God?

"I honor your gift, my friend," said Nephi, coming up on his knees. "I would like nothing more than to be able to agree to eat of it. And yet when a man has chosen the laws by which he will live, how does he choose where to draw the line, if it is not to follow the law in every whit?"

Bahram stared at him. There was no anger in his gaze. It was only a look of confusion. Finally, the sheikh struggled to his feet, and Nephi came up to meet him. The sheikh held out his hand, and Nephi took it. The sheikh placed his other sun-blackened hand over Nephi's. "My son, your words have humbled me. I have seen the power of your God. I have seen the things he has done for you, and that he loves his people. Who am I to question these things? My great apologies to you, Nephi. I would not ask you to break the laws of one who has given you so much. Indeed, I would not break them myself, in your place. I respect you the more for coming to tell me. So...what will you eat then?"

"Perhaps some of our goats."

Bahram looked about. "In time, your herds will begin to suffer. Let me send some of my people into these hills to see if they can find some beasts for the meal. It would please me."

Nephi smiled broadly. "Thank you, Father. That would please me as well."

And so it was done. Bahram sent eight of his men off on horseback to seek out and attempt to bring back goats or some other animal of which Lehi's people might partake without breaking their laws.

Nephi, back with his father and Ishmael, told them what had happened. Lehi placed his hand on the cheek of his son. "You are bound to be a great leader, a man who will be looked to for generations and whose name will be always remembered for the good. You have humbled me this day with your wisdom, and more than anything, you have filled me with great pride."

"It is the choice I think you may have made, too, in time," replied Nephi. "I learned from you."

The party lingered, visiting, in the shadows of the palms, and in the shade of a huge pavilion that the sheikh's people erected, a light gray camel and goat hair canopy held up by sturdy eight-foot-tall poles. The canopy was some thirty by forty feet, and many of the tribe and of the Jews could easily fit beneath it.

There they enjoyed the errant desert breezes, the feasting on figs and dates and other dried fruits and meats which the sheikh had brought with him. They ate cakes of flour with honey and dipped bread in olive oil and spices, and there was merriment and singing in both languages, and playing of musical instruments.

Sariah played on her large harp, one of the few worldly things she had insisted on bringing with her, which she sometimes referred to as a psaltery, a lute or a viol. The camp also rang with the sounds of the timbrel, the pipe, Lemuel's cornet, and Sam's flute, the cymbals and the tambourine. There was dancing. There was laughter. And there was peace.

It was in the evening, when the air was cooling and when stomachs were growling for the want of meat that the ceremony of the brides was held. This was the one day in a Jewish woman's life when she knew she was more important in society than her man, although any woman giving birth to a child secretly knew that she would always be the most important.

On this day, the day of marriage, the bridegroom, the *hatan*, was referred to as "king," and the bride, or *kallah*, as queen. It was most confusing to have six kings and six queens ruling Lehi's camp in the wilderness.

Even with gauzy veils before their faces, Yona and all of the daughters of Ishmael were beautiful beyond belief to their husbands. There was no formal ceremony in those days, for marriage required no state or even religious sanctions. The six brides and grooms simply stood facing each other, their hands entwined, and each spoke his or her promises to the other. The families and friends watched, and when Nephi glanced over at the sheikh his fingers were locked together in front of him, and he was surrounded by a large number of women whom Nephi presumed to be his harem. Watching, one might have believed that the daughters of Ishmael and Yona, either they or the bridegrooms, were the sheikh's own beloved offspring, for his eyes were a-glitter with tears.

Elnathan stood alone, even apart from his friends, and Yael, sister of Zoram, also was a solitary figure, and her face was wet from weeping, her hands unconsciously cradling her belly. Both Lehi and Ishmael stood with their arms around their own brides, and the smiles upon their faces could not have been brighter or larger.

Deep evening was fast wrapping the oasis of palms when the ceremony ended, and cool shadows lengthened out from the battered toes of the mountains. The moon, a huge disc of finest gold with one side sliced flat, crept up out of a crotch in the eastern mountains, and the gray-cast face etched upon it stared down at the doings in the Valley of Lemuel. Then a fine desert breeze commenced to blow, and the sands of the earth began to dance even as the people did too, and those who had instruments plied them once more, and music filled the eve.

In normal circumstances, the "king" and "queen" were now to go to the *chuppah,* the bridal chamber and also a name for the honeymoon bed, for the traditional seven days, at the end of which time they would emerge, and the feast would begin. Here in the wilderness, however, there was of course no chuppah. So the sheikh met privately with Lehi and Ishmael, and when it was decided where the proper place would be he directed his people to erect six fine tents which he had brought, and which were one of his many gifts to the people of Lehi. Lehi had professed that he was uncertain if he had enough camels to carry all that the sheikh brought, so the sheikh also gifted him with six fine new camels, one of which was a lactating female, a price beyond compare when one considered the vast importance of a single camel to a people who eked out their existence in the sands of Arabia.

And so, beginning a new tradition, the festive meal, or *seudat mitzyah,* as it was known in Hebrew, began *before* the seven days in the wedding chamber. Far into the night the dancers danced and the feasters feasted and the singers sang, and huge fires enflamed the oasis. Any danger of calling down other warring raiders was thrown aside by the sheikh himself, who had posted many armed guards around the camp. Even the camel herds, now vast with the addition of Bahram's mighty herd, roared and growled and grunted to the music, celebrating in their own comical way.

When the celebration for that night had ended, not long before the coming of dawn, the grooms led their brides away to their chuppahs, accompanied to the door by their attendants, who were chosen from the sons and daughters-in-law of Ishmael. Nephi stepped into his wedding chamber with his beautiful bride beside him, and for the first time he lowered his face and tenderly their lips met, and Rachel cried with happiness.

Nephi, smiling at his wonderful bride, softly took her up in his arms and then knelt, laying her in a bed of goat and sheep robes.

The Bedouin remained for five days, and the feasting and merriment continued. The only new visitors were of another merchant caravan passing through on their way to the north. Their appearance surprised the people of Lehi, for few seemed to know of this hidden valley and this river of water, and until now they had been left in peace. Although Bahram eyed the newly arrived merchants speculatively the peace in the valley remained, and when the caravan departed the final morning they did so in peace.

Nephi sat watching Bahram eat of the forbidden roasted camel and lick the grease from his fingers. He had never tasted camel, of course, but it smelled no different from goat, and it looked very good. For Nephi's part, he had wild goat to eat, for Bahram's sons had seen success. So there was no temptation to partake of the camel, even as young and tender as it was said to be.

Nephi and Bahram watched the merchant camel caravan departing beyond the palm trees, and Nephi eyed the sheikh, his eye corners crinkling. "You would like what they have?"

Startled, the sheikh removed his glance from the caravan to Nephi. He put his hand on his young friend's leg and smiled. "You see everything, Nephi. Is there anything that you don't see with the eyes of your God?"

Nephi laughed. "Many things, my friend. I am not certain, for one, how I merit a friend like Bahram."

The loving smile on the sheikh's face slowly disappeared as his eyes lived in Nephi's own. At last, his head turned, and he sought out someone and then found him, and he inclined his chin toward that person. "There," he said. "There is reason enough."

Nephi looked and beheld Namir, Bahram's oldest son, who had been wounded and dying when Nephi first laid eyes upon him. Namir. *"Dear."* It was a name only given to one who was very beloved, and this love gleamed like gold in the sheikh's eyes.

"You have shown unto me and to my people what it means to love, and the meaning of mercy. This I could never forget, and I could never forget the power of your God, your God of Israel, who smiles on his people more than any other god.

"That caravan, my young friend? Yes, I would have what they have. I would have their camels, I would have their women, I would have all the riches they carry. But you, Nephi, would not. You watch them go in peace, and you keep what is yours, and they keep what is theirs. I cannot say that I will never attack another caravan, for this Bedouin life that I live often leaves one no choice.

"Yet never would I make such an attack while your people are near me, for this would be a sign of deepest disrespect. And never would I go and follow and make a raid on any, such as those, who have shared my camp and shared celebration beside me. Even a Bedouin raider has to draw a line sometimes."

Nephi smiled. "Thank you, Bahram. I would that someday I might have your wisdom."

The sheikh's eyes filled with tears. "Do not even speak of my wisdom, for you make me feel lowlier than the scorpion of the sands. If I live to be eighty years old I will never have even the wisdom you possessed as a child."

Many of the wedding party were seated around a fire four nights later. By now, the feasting had slowed down, for even people who have not known much food can only bring themselves to dine for so long. The sheikh and his Bedouin were still there, but tonight they had retired early, and none of them were at the fire. This group consisted of most of Lehi's and Ishmael's families, now joined in common bond.

They were passing adventurous or comical stories around, some about events in their childhoods, some completely made up. Laman decided to entertain them all with the latest which he had heard in a tavern at Ezion-geber, and he said, "There was a woman of Edom, and she went to the market, where she bought two fish, one large and one small, one cake of figs, a little camel's milk, and some dates. A man who had been drinking wine watched her and what she was buying, and at last he looked at her with earnestness and said, 'You must not be married.' Surprised, the woman looked up at him, back to her purchases, and then at the man once more. She said, 'That is true! But how could you look at me and at what I am buying and know that I am not married?' The man said simply, 'I guessed that you are probably not married because you are really ugly!'"

Among the laughter, Sariah said, "Oh, Laman! That was not nice. Behave yourself."

But Ze'eva, Laman's bride, was laughing, and she leaned close to her man, and he squeezed her tight and kissed her cheek.

While the merriment went on, young Yael, sister of Zoram, stared into the fire. Now her brother was married, for the second time, and Yael, eighteen years old, had never interested a man in asking for her hand. Zoram had tried to tell her it was because no man wanted to approach their brute of a father, but that tale was of use for only so long. What if Laman's story applied to her as well, to Yael? What if she could find no husband because she, too, was really ugly?

She laid her hands gently on her belly, and before she knew it her lips were moving, and she was saying a prayer. It was not loud, not even loud enough for someone next to her to hear. But it did not go unnoticed.

Across the fire, Elnathan, hunter of men, was watching Yael, and his eyes were sad. Once, a long time ago, he had asked for the hand of a girl, a girl who at the time was no longer considered a girl, because she had grown so old. It had been at least two years before his bride had admitted to him that she had believed for years she was ugly, and that was why no man had wanted her hand. Elnathan smiled sadly. That woman was long gone now, dead for these many lonely years that he had remained a widower.

Yael spoke to the baby she believed to be within her. If she were indeed ugly, and that was why no man wanted her, then when it was discovered she was with child, and to her own brutal father, it would be a hundred times worse, and she would never find a man. Never. It would prove many times the reason to be unwanted. She thought of the cliffs Nephi had told her about, the cliffs that swept up high over the Red Sea. Sometimes she thought to become a bird there, to soar away, down to the crashing waves. With her she would take this tiny life that would never know a father, as she would never know a husband.

Elnathan, hunter of men, prince of Jerusalem, rose from his seat on the ground and walked around the fire. Unabashed because in the wilderness the mores of society were naught, he reached Yael, and bending down he touched her shoulder. When she looked up, he beckoned her, and hesitantly she raised her hands to him, and he lifted her up. While other eyes watched, eyes that Elnathan ignored and Yael, in her confusion, did not feel, Elnathan led Yael away from camp.

When they were standing but a ways off from the fire, Elnathan said to Yael, "It is a beautiful night for a wedding feast."

Yael was watching him, but when he said these words her eyes misted, and she looked hurriedly down. "It is indeed," she replied.

"Yael, maiden of Jerusalem, I am an old man—as old as Lehi."
He chuckled. "So I am aged only six and forty years, but that is
enough. There was a day that I would have asked your brother for
your hand, but that day is long gone."

Again, Yael's eyes fell, and for a moment it looked like she
would walk away from him.

"Now I would ask *you,*" he finished.

Yael, visibly stunned, looked up at the manhunter. It was obvious that she was rendered speechless. "I— I cannot," she said,
and she ran from the camp into the darkness.

For a long moment, Elnathan stood and looked after her. Just
when he had made up his mind to go into the darkness looking for
her, young Tikvah got up from the fire and came to him. For a
long, long time they stood in the darkness talking, and finally
Elnathan drew a deep breath, he looked after Yael, and at last he
understood many things.

"I do not know what she will think of my telling you these
things, Elnathan," said Tikvah. "But when I saw the two of you
here, and when I saw the look in her eyes, I knew I must no longer
be silent. I think I am the only one who knows. Walk softly with
Yael. She has been through more at the hands of her father than
any of us could ever know—and more than most might ever wish
to know."

Elnathan reached out and squeezed Tikvah's hands. "Thank
you. I will, as you say, walk softly."

And then into the darkness he was gone.

For a man so large, Elnathan could walk in near silence, even
as he promised, and the cushioning desert sands were his friend.
He moved in the direction Yael had gone, and he made no sound.
Thus it was that by Yael's own voice he found her, weeping in
the dark, far beyond camp and beyond the camel herd.

He breathed her name. "Please don't run from me. I would never hurt you."

He heard Yael sniffle, then all was silent but for a distant burst of laughter from camp.

Walking toward where he had heard the girl, Elnathan found her seated on the trunk of a fallen palm tree, and leaning against another. "Do you mind if I sit here next to you?"

There was no sound, so Elnathan sat, leaving a comfortable distance between them.

"I do not know how to speak what is in my heart, Yael. And I do not know how to protect your friend Tikvah while I do it. So I must say this plainly. She spoke with me after you ran away, and she has told me what your life has been, and of your fear that you carry a life inside of you, a life that is partly your father's.

"Please find no fault in Tikvah, for she wants only to help. And I think she knows me well enough to feel no fear of me. Yael, now more than ever I would be your man if you would have me. I will be the father of your child, your warrior, and your protector. No woman should face what you face alone. And no man will ever dare say a word of reproach against you, not while I am alive."

Yael was not a large woman, and Elnathan *was* a large man. Yet he almost could not stop himself from falling off the log when the girl threw herself against him, her arms around him. Yael had been praying long for a man who would accept her. Elnathan knew this deep in his heart.

There was no chuppah, no honeymoon bed or wedding chamber, for Elnathan and Yael. But it was not surprising when Nephi and Rachel gave up theirs when the wedding was announced and the ceremony performed the very next day. Elnathan had nothing of value to give for Yael, and Zoram asked nothing of him, only his strong back and his big heart, only to have Elnathan as his brother. And so the wedding feast continued with renewed vigor, and the jackals yapped an exuberant song in the folds of the rugged hills, and the sheikh and his tribe found new reason to stay on in the Valley of Lemuel.

Chapter Eleven

The Broken Bow

In time, the Bedouin said goodbye and moved on, but before they left the sheikh once again spoke with Nephi. He was still bedecked in his finery, as was his son Namir, who stood beside him in their leave-taking. Namir bowed to Nephi, and he held out before him an item about three feet long, wrapped in a finely tanned white goat skin. "This is for you, Nephi, great warrior of your God."

Bewildered, Nephi reached out and laid back the goat skin, revealing a scimitar of the most exquisite workmanship, with a gilded haft set in jewels. The blade was of the finest iron, the markings upon it intricate and fine.

"For the gift of my life this is but a token, my friend. I could never truly repay what I owe."

Embarrassed, Nephi smiled at Namir. "I wish I had something to give you in return."

"Oh, but if you did I would only have to give you something else! And the giving would never end. This is my gift in return for the gift of my life."

Then humbly Nephi bowed, and they embraced. "I will remember you fondly, Namir."

In his turn, the sheikh removed from around his neck the gaudy necklace with the huge red piece of coral set in its middle, and he motioned for Nephi to bend low. He placed the necklace around his neck, and when Nephi straightened up the sheikh admired Nephi in his new adornment. "With this necklace, and with my ring, I pray that you will always remember Bahram."

"I would always have remembered you anyway, my good friend. Until the day I die, and even beyond that day, I think."

The sheikh and Nephi embraced, and the sheikh kissed his young friend on both of his cheeks, and then he backed away and clasped his hands together in front of him, watching Nephi with sadness and joy. He climbed on his camel, made it stand, and slowly his caravan made their way back up the Valley of Lemuel, hemmed with palisades, north toward the frankincense trail.

That night in a dream the Lord came to Lehi, and his sleep was fitful. *It is time to go from this place, Lehi. On the morrow, thou and thy family will part from here and continue thy journey into the wilderness.*

The command was this simple, and it was spoken in such a way that Lehi could not question it or perceive it to be a dream of his own making.

In the morning, he awoke and lay staring at the ceiling of his tent. Sariah snored quietly beside him, and he did not have the heart to waken her. His wife had been through so much, and in his heart he knew it was going to get worse—much worse—before it got better. What trials lay before them? And how were they to bear them? Through the strength of the Lord. There was no other way.

Stepping out of his tent, Lehi was astonished to see on the ground at his feet a ball of curious, intricate workmanship. At first, he thought the Bedouin might have returned and left it for him as a gift, but as he crouched and studied it closer the Spirit of God came over him in such a way that he knew this was no mere gift of man. This was of God.

The ball was crafted of bronze, sculpted as only the finest of craftsmen could do, and it shone in the early morning light almost like a beacon. Inside the ball were two spindles, and one, shaped as an arrow, was pointing in a south-southeast direction. No matter which direction he rotated the ball, this spindle continue to maneuver around to indicate that same direction. Raising his eyes, Lehi looked that way, and a warm feeling flooded throughout his entire being. This was the way in which they were to travel.

His heart thudding loudly in his chest, Lehi took the ball in his hands, and turning to the east he fell down on his knees and praised the Lord. For many minutes Lehi prayed until he felt a presence near him of more than just the Lord. Looking up, he saw Nephi standing several feet away, watching him. He did not understand completely how, but he realized at that moment that Nephi had already known they were leaving. Nephi had seen the ball, he had felt the Lord's presence here, and he came to Lehi and helped him to his feet.

Before Lehi could speak, Nephi said, "I was wakened, Father, and told to come here to your tent. This thing, it is of the Lord."

Lehi looked down at the ball, and his hands were trembling. "Yes, my son. We are leaving, and from here on I know not where, except that this ball has told us to travel in that direction." He pointed. "I know only that the Lord will guide us."

And so they gathered all that they had over the next two days, including all of the seeds of every kind that they had sowed and harvested, the six new camels, the three horses and the tents which had been a gift from the Bedouin, and all of their kin, and they set out to the south-southeast, in the direction shown them by their new and strange compass, known in their language as a *liahona*. It gave Nephi a sad and lonesome feeling in his heart to look back upon the wonderful place they had known for so long as a home, but another feeling of wonder and peace glowed within him as he looked at the way ahead. They were on to the promised land.

The days became fiercely hot, and the landscape at many times, beyond an isolated acacia tree or a brittle bush or clump of grass here or there, utterly barren, so that when they pitched their tents again, four days later, everyone was miserable, and they were glad for a rest. The water in the last two nights' camps had been severely brackish, and only by adding sour camel milk were they able to consume it. They had a little dried meat Bahram's people had given them, but otherwise they subsisted on dried dates, berries, raisins and some figs, sparing as much of their grain as possible for seed for their final destination. For liquid nourishment, they drank of camel milk, and every now and then Laman and Lemuel and the sons of Ishmael would pass about their wine, but that was growing scarce.

The desert here, especially along the highlands, could be surprisingly humid, more so than any of the women or children had ever experienced, not having journeyed forth in the Arabian desert before. At times, with the high temperature and high humidity, they found it hard to breathe, and they began to find traveling at night, or early in the mornings and late in the evenings, the only travel possible. They continued to give much thanks to the Lord for the liahona, for traveling through the deep dark of these desert nights could not have been done without it.

Here in the new place where they pitched their tents the mountains about them seemed to twist and intertwine, as did many game trails that wandered past. For that reason they called the place Shazer, which in Hebrew meant just what this place appeared to do: twist and intertwine.

From their base camp, Nephi, Sam, Laman and Lemuel went into the mountains with their bows to obtain game. Even Elnathan and his comrades, Lotan, Zoram, and all the sons of Ishmael took slings and stones and tried to gather whatever food they could find. Unfortunately, most of what they could find and could have killed were hares and rabbits and other animals specifically forbidden in the book of Leviticus to be partaken of by man, because they were unclean. What the slings and stones could harvest of grouse and partridges was slim, yet anything would be of help in the great, vast desert ahead.

With his fine steel bow, which was a composite bow made partly of wood, partly of steel, Nephi brought down three oryx and an ibex over the five days they hunted. The bow was designed to be a long range weapon, and many hours of practice in the hills around Jerusalem had made of him an expert bowman. With his own skill in aiming and lightly letting his arrows fly, and the Lord's help in finding game, he felt competent to bring home game meat, even if the only shots he was presented were fifty yards or more away.

Laman, Lemuel and Sam, with their composite bows of wood, brought down one animal each, but they had all started noticing their weapons did not seem as powerful as they had before, and when they all gathered together at night with their game, Nephi began looking their bows over. The spring in the bows seemed weak, and Nephi wondered if it had something to do with the great humidity and heat of this place. Could it be weakening the wood, slowly rendering the wooden bows useless? Or had his brothers simply become careless and been neglectful in keeping the wood well-oiled? Either way, it could be disastrous.

A chill passed over Nephi, and again he looked to the wood of his own bow, frowning in deep thought.

Well, it did not matter. The Lord had brought them here, and the Lord would provide. They would not soon make it through these vast deserts without him.

They returned to camp and cut up most of their game in thin strips to dry it, then laid it around on rocks, on canvas, or on whatever they could find. The humidity was of no help, but in spite of it the heat of the days was so great that in short time, and with enough of the salt they had brought with them, the meat was cured, and they were ready once more to travel.

It was prior to leaving Shazer that Sariah broke to the entire camp her wonderful news: She, although of the advanced age of eight and thirty years, was with child, and she believed she had been for two months now. There was a great celebration in camp that night.

Only because of the liahona, for Lehi was not familiar with these wastes through which they traveled now, were they able to travel in the more fertile parts of the wilderness, in the "borders," or mountains, near the Red Sea, where thanks to the Lord and the liahona there was always enough graze for the camels, horses, sheep and goats and just enough water for all, even if the water was not always very good.

They traveled on for many days, slaying food along the way as they found it. But the humidity and heat, for such they had decided was the cause of it, had rendered the wooden bows nearly useless, so that they had to rely only on slings and stones and on Nephi's powerful steel bow.

The heat of the desert continued brutal. It bore down on them, seeming to bake them even through their clothing, which they kept almost entirely covering themselves like shrouds. The sand was ferociously hot, and it would creep up between their sandals and their feet when they walked, and it would blister their heels and their toes, so great was its heat.

On and on they traveled, and the water was bad, and their lips began to crack and to bleed, and their throats were parched. The water, as bad as it was, was precious, and they had to drink sparingly, so that in time their tongues began to feel swollen, and there was little talk as they slogged on through the sand and over the barren wastes of stone and dried, cracked mud.

At last, they found a place at the heels of the mountains where they could take rest, a place with trees and oleander bushes and fruit-bearing shrubs whose fruit had unfortunately dried and fallen to the ground or been eaten by animals or birds.

Here again they pitched their tents, which were already plagued with swarms of fleas that had followed them from their last camp. They looked to the high mountains near them, where even through the shimmering heat it appeared there might be timber, after a fashion, very high up, and there they hoped for game, for what they had already killed and dried was now growing scarce.

If it was indeed timber shimmering distant blue-gray on the mountains, as it seemed, it was the first that they could refer to as such that they had seen in many weeks.

Only Nephi, Sam and Lotan and Elnathan's men went out with good hearts on the hunt this time. Laman and Lemuel, Shedrar and Yavin went, but not with good hearts. They were worn and weary and were beginning once more to murmur about the harsh conditions and to wish they could be back in Jerusalem. The other young men did not even bother to go out, but remained, in their words, to protect those in camp.

Nephi split off from the others, climbing high into the broken, sun-beaten peaks where the graceful bull oryx with their long, black, elegant horns liked to hide. It was toward mid-afternoon when he heard a sound, and looking ahead he saw a beautiful oryx that had bounded from its bed and stood looking at him, only forty yards away.

Bachelor oryx were inevitably solitary animals, by some un-written law of their own kind, and by the looks of this one he had been around some time. So Nephi did not even bother looking for a more tender animal to shoot. It was evident that God had gifted him with this one.

The Arabian oryx boasts of a beautiful white hide to reflect the sun, with long, ringed, almost straight horns, in the case of this old male some two or more feet long. This one probably weighed all of two hundred seventy pounds, huge for his kind. He had the chocolate-brown legs, the black cheek patches, and the upside down black triangle on the bridge of his nose that marked all of his breed. For longer than he should have, Nephi admired the beautiful beast that the Lord had offered him, watching him flick his large ears and stare curiously at the hunter. It made Nephi sad, in a way, to put down such a magnificent animal, but the Lord had done his part, and now it was up to Nephi to provide for his family.

With thanks to the Lord, he drew back his bow string.

What happened next was so shocking that for a moment Nephi just gawked, first at his hand, and then up at the oryx, which stood there staring at him, its eyes full of nothing more than mild curiosity. Nephi had struck himself in the face so hard it felt as if someone had punched him viciously, and his cheek began to swell up and to throb with pain. Looking down, he saw that his steel bow had broken! When he had pulled it almost all the way back and was set to release it, it had snapped. He had had to pull back very hard on the bowstring for the stout bow to reach the farthest point of its arc, and, with the sudden snap of the steel, his hand had continued on in a direct line, in the form of a fist, slamming him in the face.

He was still holding the arrow in his right hand, the broken bow in his left, when he felt blood start running down his lip from his nose, and the oryx turned and slowly sauntered away, conserving its own energy yet having no further reason to stay and trade stares with this strange creature who faced it.

With sadness in his heart, Nephi watched the mighty oryx disappear at last into a fold in the hills, then returned to the place he and the others had appointed to meet. Elnathan and his young, stout comrade Ilai were already there, and they got stricken looks upon their faces when Nephi, his cheek and nose badly swollen, lifted his bow wordlessly for them to see the dangling broken end of it. Slowly, the others came in, and only Sam brought any game with him. This was but a large partridge—for close to thirty people to feed on.

Laman, Lemuel, Shedrar and Yavin straggled in last, and none of them had anything to show for their day's hunt. They looked around those gathered until their eyes settled with hope on Nephi. Then Laman's eyes fell on the steel bow, which lay at his feet.

Laman started, then took a few steps forward. It was as if he did not believe, or at least did not wish to believe, what he was seeing. "Nephi! What did you do?"

"I tried to shoot an oryx," said Nephi simply, and shrugged. "When I drew back, it broke."

Laman looked at Nephi's swollen cheek as Lemuel came up behind him on the left, and Shedrar and Yavin at his right shoulder. They all stared in dismay at Nephi's bow, the last useful bow among them.

"You have done well, Nephi!" growled Shedrar derisively. "Now what do we do, eat camel droppings?"

"Yes, if you don't curb your tongue," growled Elnathan, and No'ach puffed out his chest beside his friend to throw his weight into that threat as well.

"Perhaps instead of complaining to Nephi you should have brought a bow of your own," growled No'ach. "Or maybe Laman and Lemuel might have kept the wood of their own bows properly oiled."

"The law is going to be severely ignored, I think," said Lemuel, ignoring Elnathan's and No'ach's comments. "We are not to eat animals such as rabbits, yet I have seen more rabbits than of anything else in these mountains. And scorpions and serpents as well. If the Lord truly did not want us to eat of rabbits and hares, scorpions and serpents, then why would he show us only these?"

"There is plenty of game here," said Ishmael's youngest son, Yavin. "For a man with a bow. Nephi, if you had kept grease on that bow as you should have perhaps it would not have broken."

"Yes, Nephi, what of that?" Laman stooped and swept up the broken bow. He studied it for a moment, and although for the most part the steel was clean and unmarred, where it had broken it had been against the wood, and on the back side, which had been hidden tight against the wood, it was plain where the humid air and the heat of the desert had gotten to it and had begun to corrode the metal. This was where it had broken.

"Corroded by rust!" Shedrar sang out triumphantly. "I can see it from here. I should have taken your bow from you long ago and kept it for myself. You cannot treat a fine weapon like it will last forever without care."

"Hush your mouths!" came Elnathan's angry voice. He lunged forward and jerked the bow out of Laman's hand. "Look at this! You can see that where the bow rusted there was no way to get grease to it. It would have had to go between the wood and the steel, and there was no way to get it there. It was only a matter of time. I will not stand by while the four of you badmouth the only man of you of any worth, especially when you all could so easily have saved your own bows by keeping oil on them. Stay your evil tongues. The Lord might not strike you down, but I will."

Laman and Lemuel, Yavin and Shedrar would only stare up at Elnathan, who seemed even larger in his rage. At last, Laman turned on his heel, and without a word he started back down the mountain. Of course, Lemuel went with him, and shortly after, Yavin and Shedrar. A minute later, Nephi walked over to Elnathan, and from his hand he took the remnants of his magnificent bow, which had cost him dearly at the market, and which he had treasured above almost all of his worldly possessions.

Frowning in deep thought, he studied the bow for a long time, then at last unfastened its string, rolled it and put it in his pouch, and with a fling sent the bow over the edge of a precipice. They could hear it *clink* and *clank* for quite some time as it bounced over the rocks into oblivion.

"Thank you, my friend," Nephi said to Elnathan as the rest of them stood there quietly. "Come. We had best go back to camp, and it would not hurt to get there not long after my brothers. You never know what trouble they will have stirred up if we let them arrive long ahead of us."

Elnathan grabbed Nephi's shoulder and turned him back around as he was about to walk away. "I have nothing but trust in you, Nephi. You will find a way through this, or no man can."

The hike back down the mountains was quiet. No one spoke a word, and it was just beginning to sink in to them what kind of dire situation they might be in now. They had the smoked and salted dried meat from their earlier successes, but with so many people eating of it it could not last long. And the sacks of different grains and seeds they had amassed would serve no purpose as food, for it would be gone in a short time with almost thirty mouths to nourish, and then they would be left with no seed to plant for their future.

Without the hand of the Lord, starvation was now imminent— immediately, if they chose not to eat the grain and seeds, or later, if they did.

Chapter Twelve

A Bow and a Single Arrow

The time came when the voice of the Lord whispered quietly to Lehi's people to be easy with fire, by day or by night. The presence of warring tribes and wild animals made it too dangerous. Many merchant caravans had been overrun and taken captive or killed in this desert. Lehi and Ishmael, having taken many a trading caravan in the past, and having seen many that did not return, knew these dangers. So when God spoke to them about avoiding fire, they understood. It was a step necessary to keep them safe.

Generally, before leaving on such an expedition as theirs, a man would settle his affairs, such were the chances of not coming back. And many of the richer merchants would hire men to take their caravans out for them, knowing the severe risks they faced. Lehi's people now would be especially vulnerable to attack because of all the women with them, which raiders would covet for wives, and the children, who would serve well as slaves.

So as evening fell they had to leave their tents and find a place up in the shelter of rocks where they could soften some of their dried meat by soaking it in a pot. The entire clan of Lehi and Ishmael gathered there, and there was no peace to be had among them this night. As usual, Laman and Lemuel and the sons of Ishmael clamored to retrace their steps back to Jerusalem, and most of their women were either silent or in full agreement with them. What surprised Nephi was that even Lehi said little against them. Lehi, who had begun in the last few weeks to seem tired and old, sat in silence and listened to the voices of his sons and his sons-in-law, and he stared at the sand, his shoulders sagging. The nearly constant dissension in camp was wearing down this man of once endless strength and courage.

Ishmael, who had begun to show signs of his ailment again even before the feasting had ended and the Bedouin had left their camp, was also silent, and he and Ra'ya left the gathering and returned to their tent before dusk had settled deep in the valley.

Besides Sam, the four most vocal of those who spoke on Nephi's side were four that anyone looking on might have thought should have no great say in any affair of the Lehi-Ishmael camp, and these were Zoram, Elnathan, No'ach and Lotan. Zoram was the first to stand, pushing up from where Ginath was nestled in his arms.

"I am in shame for you, the sons of Ishmael and Laman and Lemuel, who should know better after all you have seen. You sons of Lehi, I was in Jerusalem when you came for the plates of brass, and there I witnessed the strength that was in Nephi. I felt the mighty power of the Lord, and you did as well. This is something that unless you lie you cannot deny.

"I know nothing of Nephi having been chosen to be your leader. It is you who continue to speak of this, and although it seems only reasonable after watching the lot of you quarrel, for all I know, Laman, if you were to repent and follow the voice of the Lord perhaps he would appoint you a leader over all of Lehi's people after Lehi is no more.

"What I know I know simply of where we stand now. It is faith in God, and a knowledge that he is leading us to a promised land that has gotten us this far. I do not know whither we go, but I believe that our chances of going there are as good as our chances of returning to Jerusalem. And we know what awaits us in Jerusalem—certain death. Or captivity, which is worse!"

"Do we?" Laman jumped up and shouted angrily. "Do we indeed? It is only the word of our father and of Nephi that tells us death or captivity awaits us in Jerusalem. You know nothing of this, no more than do I. Or has the Lord spoken to you now as well, Zoram? It is funny, but it seems as if he chooses to speak to everyone who believes in our father."

A moment of silence followed, while Zoram and Laman stared each other down, and the dim shadows danced. "In days of old, in a situation such as this, the Lord spoke to his people through the prophet Moses. The Lord speaks to me today through another prophet, Laman—your father. I need nothing more. We know what happened when the children of Israel failed to heed Moses's voice. Furthermore, the death that awaits some of us awaits us because of the things that have been done by us in Jerusalem—treason, thievery against the king . . . and murder."

Angrily, Laman scoffed, kicking sand. He could not deny the truth of these words. He looked over quickly at Lehi, but the older man was studying the sand at his feet. Laman took strength from this.

"You are a weak old woman, Zoram, blinded by lies of wonderful things that do not exist. You follow Nephi because you need a figure who appears to be strong, someone who can lead you so you do not have to think for yourself. You will live to regret this, as has every weak man in history."

"You mean the way the children of Noah followed him?" retorted Zoram.

"No matter whom we follow," cut in Shedrar, rising to his feet, "the fact is we will all starve to death if we do not find a way to get food. Let us be honest with each other. We can go neither forward nor back to Jerusalem now on the amount of food in this camp. That is all you need to think about, Zoram, no matter whom you choose to follow. No matter whom you convince yourself is a prophet hearing the words of God."

With that, Shedrar stalked off in the direction his parents had gone, and slowly the others straggled after.

At last, it was Nephi and Lehi left standing alone, and the blue and lonesome darkness began to close like a pall over them. Nephi put up a hand and rested it on Lehi's shoulder. "Fear not, Father. I sense a deep distress in you, and I know that you grieve because you think it is your fault that we are in this situation."

"Nephi, my family is going to starve, and I am helpless to do anything about it. Shedrar was right: We cannot go forward in the direction the liahona points, nor can we go back, for either way, without nourishment that can only be brought down with bows, is sure death."

"What does your heart tell you?" asked Nephi.

"That is why I feel so weary, my son. My heart is telling me nothing. The voice of the Lord has gone still."

And so the camp of Lehi suffered, staying put in this place where they had pitched their tents, at the feet of the mighty mountains and not very far from the shores of the main body of the Red Sea (for long since they had left behind the Gulf of Aqabah). They feared to go on into the unknown, but knowing already the vast desert behind them they could not bring themselves to go back. The valley where they had stopped was at least semi-fertile, and here was water, so that they could plant a crop, which they did.

Sadly, however, Lehi and his people planted the crop with little faith that anything would come of it, for they did not trust this water source far.

And the days went by, and the murmuring grew louder and more angry, and even Lehi began to murmur against the Lord because of the suffering of his family. Sam remained faithful, watching to Nephi for a sign that help would come, and Rachel remained always by her husband, always his helpmate. In time, only Rachel, Zoram, Elnathan, No'ach, Yael, Lotan, Yona, Sam and Ariel were in support of Nephi, and all of the others were ready to try to make it back home as opposed to staying in this valley, this *wadi*, of impending death.

The humidity began to take its toll on them, for it made the heat seem doubly stifling. The sand was like a fire pit in the day, and the biting cold swept down at night, when there could be no fires, and gnawed against their bones. Wolves began to howl about the camp at night, and there were times that Ishmael's sons contemplated going out with spears and trying to kill them, for even the meat of wolves could not be as bad as hearing the withering cries and witnessing the starvation of their young ones. They had come to be of the opinion that whatever animal presented itself, if they had a chance they would kill and eat it, for if the Lord did not provide "clean" animals for them then they must survive on those designated "unclean."

They began to wonder if they should not have saved some of the seeds they had planted, saved them either for planting in some other place or to eat. For although they had begun to sprout, there was no sure sign that they would mature in time to serve as a food source.

Then Nephi, watching his family and his friends suffer, knew it was up to him once more. Up to him to bring them through, to bring back the faith to them and to bring nourishment to their stomachs. So he took himself up into the mountain and he prayed, and when he returned to Lehi's camp the Spirit of God was upon him, and he was not afraid.

"I am come from praying in the mountain," Nephi announced over a breakfast of thin broth and boiled goat meat. "The Lord has told me to make a bow and arrows."

There was a long silence in the camp, and then a few half-hearted snickers. Finally, Laman and some of the others laughed outright. "Make a bow! Nephi, you are a fool," his oldest brother said. "There is no wood here to make a bow, and if there were it would not matter, for you do not know how."

Lemuel laughed at his brother's words, and Shedrar, Hidai, Gera and Yavin looked appropriately disgusted. Tikvah simply looked at her brother with sadness, yet with hope. She did not like the way her husband treated Nephi, but she had long since stopped daring say anything against it. She only prayed that Nephi's words could be true, for they all needed something to believe in now.

"I do not need to know how, brother," replied Nephi. "The Lord will make all things possible. I will make a bow. But I would say other things to you before I go from here. The Lord is sore unhappy with how his people murmur—his people, whom he saw fit to bring out of the land of Jerusalem, out of bondage—away from destruction. He brought all of us here so that we might find a new promised land, a land where we might raise our families, a land where we might find hope. Like the people of Moses of old, we are being tested, and the Lord is unhappy with what he has seen of us. In spite of all the great signs he has shown us, still we murmur and talk of going back to Jerusalem, although that road is truly hopeless. I am going to the mountain, where I will make me a new bow and arrows, which the Lord will guide me in doing. And I pray that some of you here in camp will find a reason to pray to your God and ask for forgiveness, and ask that you might go forward without murmuring from here forth, that you might be forgiven of your weaknesses."

He did not intend for his glance to be at his father, yet it was, and Lehi met his eyes with much sadness and was still watching him solemnly as Nephi turned and hiked away.

Nephi let the Spirit of the Lord guide him as he climbed the mountain. He remembered seeing a thick grove of some kind of tree he did not know, high on the point of a mountain as he was hunting, and this was the general direction in which he traveled.

It was early in the afternoon when he reached a deep, humbling canyon, the jaws, as of death, that opened with jagged teeth and remorseless, ragged throat that dared him to cross to the other side. On the other side he could see the grove of trees he remembered. There were only perhaps forty or fifty of them, all growing closely together.

And the voice of the Lord came to Nephi's heart and told him he must cross this canyon of threatening death, so Nephi started across it wearing the armor of the Lord.

Battered and weary, bleeding and bruised, Nephi finally made his way over the highest lip of the far canyon, and there before him ranked the grove of trees. The day now was growing late, and the shadows stretched out from their trunks toward him as if reaching out to embrace him. With new strength, he sipped of a goat skin of water, and then he walked reverently among the trees, trees the like of which he had never seen before. These trees were tall and straight, some of them forty feet high. But among them were also young ones, with slim, supple trunks, and as he walked among them and his hands fondled the smooth bark, it felt as if one of the trees were calling to him. A strange power seemed to shake this young tree to its very height, and a strength he could only believe was from the Lord coursed out of its bark and into his trembling hands.

With a prayer of thanks, Nephi took his axe and hewed down the tree, and for some time he sat in the grove and stroked the smooth bark and spoke softly to the tree, thanking it, as he thanked the Lord, for offering its life to him and his people.

The trunk of the tree was about twice as big around as Nephi's wrist, and it was well over tall enough to make a bow of Nephi's height, with good, solid, knot-less wood all the way. As the Lord guided Nephi's hands he began to cut away at the trunk with his axe, and then, when he had taken away enough wood with the axe, he turned to the knife.

Nephi, with no nourishment inside him, only water, carved and smoothed and studied his bow-in-the-making, from time to time saying an earnest prayer and holding it out away from him to look at it carefully from tip to tip, measuring it for exactness and balance. He could feel the Lord's hand guiding him every step of the way.

With memory of his own bow of steel in mind, he crafted and shaped this new bow, yet he kept the limbs stouter, as they would not have the advantages of a composite bow, and the spirit and his common sense told him they must be thicker to keep from breaking off.

When at last evening fell, Nephi was still on the mountain, and there was no descending that awful chasm in the dark. So he nestled down in the rocks and drew his goat skins around his torso as tightly as he could, and then he said a prayer of thanks to the Lord and settled in for a long night.

Nephi was blessed with sound sleep, and in the morning he awoke ready to start on his bow again. But now his fingers ached mightily from gripping the bow and the knife, and he had to stretch them out and rub them vigorously to get them to work for him again. At last, first feebly, he was able to start on the carving once more, only now it was more of an effort of smoothing than of actual carving.

Two hours later, he held up his bow, and a rush of power sped through his entire body, making bumps rise up on his flesh and tears dim his eyes. This was his bow! A bow straight from the hand of God! He carefully carved grooves near the ends of both farthest points, as he remembered them to be on his steel bow, and then he took the string he had kept in his pouch from his steel bow and fastened it to the new bow. Rather than string it the way it seemed natural, the spirit told him to bend the bow backward, and when he drew back the string to his eye he felt an incomparable strength inside this weapon.

As it turned out, making an arrow was almost as much work as making the bow itself, for there were no small, slender sticks to use for the purpose, and he had to cut down a tree as big around as his thumb and then carefully whittle it down until it was as straight as he could make it, then attach one of his bronze arrow-heads, those which he had used with his first bow.

Lastly, he used heated pitch to glue shed hawk feathers he had found while hiking to the end of the arrow shaft for fletching, that which would make it fly true, and he wrapped that with sinew and also glued it in place with the pitch.

Because it was well into the day now, instead of making other arrows he was directed to hunt with only this one. It took a huge amount of faith to stand up and prepare to leave with only one arrow to rely on, but as the spirit directed he cut down nine young trees to take with him, then got down on his knees.

With all his might and all his spirit, Nephi prayed and thanked the Lord for helping him construct the bow and the arrow, and he prayed that his single arrow would fly true. At last, he started home.

It was dark before he arrived.

Chapter Thirteen

Death in a
Place Called Nahom

In the quiet of the camp, Nephi moved, listening intently to the sounds of the night. The camels snuffled in the darkness, looking for grass to eat, and in one of the tents a woman sang softly to a child. Another child laughed, and a man's voice spoke soothing words. There was not one sound from any of the dogs or the horses or other stock.

"Nephi?"

For some reason, the voice from the dark failed to startle him, and Nephi looked toward the shadows where his friend Zoram lurked. "It is I."

Zoram came forward in a rush, embracing the man who was more like a brother than a friend. "We have feared for you. Are you hungry?"

Nephi laughed. "No, not hungry, brother Zoram. The Lord has fed me well upon his spirit."

"Some are ready to go home tomorrow," said Zoram. "They have lost all faith and are ready to brave the path behind us rather than to go forward into the unknown."

"Laman and Lemuel?"

Nephi could barely see Zoram nodding in reply. "Yes, but Shedrar is the worst. And even one of the friends of Elnathan—Reuven. He has started to stay with your brothers and with the sons of Ishmael, and he grows vicious in the words he speaks. I have often wondered about those men and where they would side if things got bad for us."

Nephi was saddened to hear this about Reuven, for he had never felt any reason not to trust him—him, nor any of the other friends of Elnathan. He hoped this was not the beginning of something bad for all of them.

"I have made me a bow of wood, and an arrow," announced Nephi. "Tomorrow I will bring back meat, and if you will accompany me to help carry it I would be much pleased."

"Good, brother!" said Zoram excitedly. "I will be up before the dawn. I knew that your faith would save us all."

Nephi smiled in the dark, for it warmed his heart that Zoram made no mention of the fact that he had only one arrow. He leaned forward and down until his forehead rested against Zoram's, and his hand lay on the back of his neck. "I am able to go on because I feel your friendship and that of a few others, Zoram. I pray you will always believe."

In the morning, Nephi rose before first light and went to the tent of his father. Without invitation, he went into the tent and shook his father lightly and bade him to come with him outside.

"I have made a bow of wood, Father, and I will obtain food for us today. I would have you show me where I must go to obtain this food."

After a long silence, Lehi's hand closed on Nephi's arm. "My son, I did not believe in you. Why would you ask *me* now for help?"

"You are my father, and my prophet, he who heard the voice of the Lord which has saved us all from the destruction of Jerusalem. Who else would I come to, Father?"

Lehi fought to choke back his emotions and Nephi was glad for his father that it was still dark. At last, Lehi said, "I will pray, my son. Blessed be ye for your faith. I will pray, and then I will come for you."

After Nephi had gone, Lehi crouched in silence at the door of his tent. His heart was pounding soddenly, and it was heavy with grief. He had let down the Lord. He had let down his people. And now it was his youngest son who had to bring him back to faith. He had been so ready to give up, and yet Nephi remained steadfast. How was this so?

After some time of humbling himself in his heart, Lehi was able to bow his head and begin to pray, and he asked first for forgiveness and for the strength that God had granted his son. The strength was some time in coming. Beforehand, Lehi endured much in the way of chastening. He was chastised for his murmuring, chastised for losing faith, and chastised for giving way to the complaints of his sons and the sons of Ishmael when these people looked to him more than anyone to be their source of spiritual strength.

Finally, with tears pouring down his cheeks, Lehi said out loud, "Please, Lord, give me strength and forgiveness, and I will never weaken more."

The shaking in his frame ceased, and a feeling of utter peace flooded down over his entire body. Lehi crouched there, spent, but waiting to hear further instructions from God. At last, he heard the words, *Look upon the ball, and behold the things which are written.*

By now, a gray light had come over the camp, and others were stirring about. There was a strange power emanating from the earth, or the sky, or from where no one knew for certain, but everyone felt it, and it made the people rise from their beds to find out what this strange spirit was.

Lehi went into his tent, and he came out with Sariah behind him and was holding before him the liahona, which seemed to be glowing softly of its own power. Everyone had gathered around Lehi's tent, feeling that strange power drawing them there, a power which could not be refused. Lehi looked into the ball, at the spindles which were inside of it, and he began to tremble once more.

Upon the spindles were written words, words which were plain to read. And these spindles, in the beginning, had been smooth and clear, with no mark upon them. And all who had seen them, even Laman and Lemuel, knew this to be true.

Lehi was too stunned to read out loud what the spindles said, so he simply passed the ball around from person to person, and all read. The words were plain to be understood: *And if thy faith be simple and pure as that of a child, this compass shall lead ye in the way that ye should go. Yet if ye shall falter ye shall see no sign upon it, and your way shall not be as a window, but as a wall.*

All who looked upon the words, especially those who had murmured against the word of God, shook mightily and fell on their knees in prayer. And the power of God swept over the camp of Lehi like a mighty, rushing wind.

Nephi went into the mountains with his brothers and his friends, and by the power of Nephi's faith, coupled with the direction given him by his father, he was guided to game that hid itself in the highest reaches and in the canyons. Early in the day, not far from camp, he slew a large male oryx, and when he went to retrieve his arrow he saw the unbelievable: This big male, which should have been a loner, was not alone! A female was standing only thirty paces away, watching him. With all his care, he withdrew the arrow, which was so well made that the arrowhead remained intact, and the Lord guided his eye in a second shot. The female ran only forty yards away before stopping and then keeling over. In less than two minutes, and with the same arrow, he had two full grown oryx lying dead on the ground. The two animals required Elnathan and his three friends to carry them down the mountain in halves.

Later, using the same arrow, Nephi killed an ibex standing at the edge of a precipice with a shot in the neck, and this, too, was large enough that two men had to carry it away. Nephi was left with Sam, Lotan, Laman and Lemuel.

Laman and Lemuel had nothing to say as a second ibex, which had stayed close by where its mate had fallen even after the rest of the herd had vanished higher in the rocks, was slain with the same arrow that had killed its mate and the pair of oryx. There was nothing they *could* say, for they were greatly shamed for the way they had murmured, yet their pride was still too strong for them to apologize to their younger brother. Perhaps the time of apologies had passed.

The camp of Lehi rose up in great celebration that evening, and Lehi spoke to them in humility and promised that he would never more let his faith falter. They ate the meat raw, for fear of bringing down marauders with the light of cooking fires, but by the power of God, as he had promised Lehi in a dream, the meat was made soft and sweet. Even the brackish water seemed almost sweet that night.

There was dancing, and there was singing, and there was prayer.

But for Ishmael, it was not a time of celebration. He sat back in the shadows and watched the merrymaking of his family, of his sons, his daughters, his grandchildren. But deep in Ishmael's chest was a pain that would not go away, and it gnawed at him and pressed against his breastbone, and at times his arm ached, and sometimes his jaw. He sat and wondered what caused the pain, and if he dared ask Lehi or Nephi for a blessing from God. Yet somehow, he knew this was not to be so, for something whispered to him in his heart, asking him to say goodbye to those he loved.

He looked toward Ra'ya, his sweet wife. She was cradling one of the young ones, and she seemed so happy. She looked for all the world like a girl of twenty-five, and yet Ishmael felt to be seventy. How had he aged so, when others around him stayed so young? He was sad, yet he was happy, for he could not truly have expected to live to the age he had, and he was grateful.

In time, the grains had all ripened, and they were harvested. Then all was made ready, and the people of Lehi struck their tents and traveled on, in nearly the same direction they had traveled before, in the direction the liahona bade them go. This time they could only rely on Nephi's bow for food, and on the slings of the others, but they were blessed of the Lord, and always they found the nourishment they sought.

Yet the red sands seemed so fiery, and the sun blasted down, and even the camels complained. The horses and the remainder of the sheep and goats, however, plodded along in silence, for they had not the strength even to raise a voice of woe.

Some of their days seemed to go on forever, and the temperatures reached up over one hundred twenty degrees in the open sun. These times they were forced to travel only in the very early morning, before dawn, and then beginning late in the afternoon until deep in the night and then rely on the noses of the camels not to pass by the watering places. Those nights, they would simply fall on the ground and sleep, wrapped in their own clothing, too tired to eat or to make a bed. They could only drink and then lie down, and sometimes they barely had the strength to pray, to thank the Lord for helping them through another day.

The ragged, sandy wastes seemed endless. The sun was like a ball of molten brass, and it scorched every bit of their skin that was exposed as if molten rays were breaking loose from it and descending to earth. Their eyes burned and the whites of them were red, and they plodded on, their ears ringing with the heat, their tongues swelling for lack of moisture, and thought only of whatever water lay ahead—praying that there would indeed be water.

Even the camels, long-suffering beasts that they were, seemed to step forward only out of habit, as dead things brought to temporary life. Their eyes were often half shut now, whether the wind was blowing or whether the day was fiery and still. They had ceased to grunt, except when an occasional one escaped them by accident, and they had long since tired of nipping at each other, of switching their tails, of shaking their heads to listen to the rattle of their reins. Even in camp, when they would normally have been scratching against tree trunks to fight against the tireless, marauding fleas that plagued them day and night, the camels just stood listless or wandered from clump to clump of grass, their humps shrunk up now from lack of food and proper moisture, and often slumping to one side as they did after long periods of drought. As for the horses, sheep and goats, had it not been for the water in the skins the camels were bearing, they, like the people, would long since have been dead.

Finally, they came to an oasis that gave them hope, where the water was pure and the trees were tall. Oleander bushes were in flower, and a small flock of ibises took off from the water at their approach.

Here, it was decided that they would stay for quite some time, and that they must once again try to plant a crop, so they used much of the seed they had harvested from their last crop and started anew, following a path of faith. The rainy season began once more, and the crops began to sprout, and each day the mists came, and the valley bloomed and was beautiful with waving flowers.

In this place of rest, a boy child was born to Zoram's sister Yael, and Elnathan claimed it as his own and would let no man openly question the date of its conception. They named it Barak, meaning "Lightning," and from the very beginning the child was strong and ill-tempered.

A month later there was also a child born to Sariah, and they named this boy Jacob, and in temperament he was the exact opposite of the son of Yael. Jacob was dark of hair like his brothers, and steady of eye, but he was quick to smile and quick to squeeze a finger when it was proffered him.

It was in this camp, also, that it was learned there would be many more mouths to feed, for all of the daughters of Ishmael, even his eldest, Ginath, the wife of Zoram, became great with child in this fruitful valley—at least fruitful in the way of human-kind. Of the newly married, left to become pregnant was only Yona, who in her heart began to wonder, after Ginath announced her own condition, if she would ever be blessed with a child. It was always the great fear of the woman of that day not to be able to bless her husband with a child. Often, as was the case with Yona, the wife began to wonder if she failed to conceive because she had done something to offend the Lord.

Some years passed in this place, as they sowed and reaped their many grains more than once, and the water source held strong. Nephi, reaching the age of twenty-three grew here to his full stature, his torso and his legs filling out, his jaw growing and hardening like a rock. Inspired of the Lord, he would go often-times into the mountain there not only to pray but for an increase of strength to repeatedly lift heavy stones, as he had so often done in his childhood. He would pick them up off the ground, some-times curl them up toward his chin. Other times he would press them over his head or let them slowly lower to a place behind his neck, then bring them back up again. And in these years the might of Nephi grew to such an extent that those who loved him began to call him "the Ox," a name by which he had sometimes teasingly been called in his younger days. Now it fit.

In this very place, as well, the family grew. When five years had gone by, Laman and Ze'eva had been blessed with three chil-dren, two boys and one girl, Neco, Seth, and Ruth; Lemuel and

Yaakova with two daughters, Heqet and Nike; Sam and Ari'el with a son and a daughter, Raphael and Tirzah; Nephi and Rachel with one daughter and two sons, Rebekah, Zur, and Ethan; Zoram and Ginath with two daughters, Rhode and Chava; Joab and Zipporah with another son and a daughter, Peleg and Yemima; Shedrar and Tikvah with a daughter and a second son, Tauwret and Jarib; and Elnathan and Yael with another son and a daughter, Little Nephi and Little Rachel.

The other five sons of Ishmael and their wives also continued to have babies, and in time many small voices filled the camp.

And to the delight and surprise of all, Sariah conceived once more, and in the sixth year of their escape from the land of Jerusalem she gave birth to a healthy boy they christened Joseph.

With all of the conception and birth-giving going on around them in this place, and having watched only one baby out of them all die, due to some condition with which it was born, this which would have been the fourth baby of Tikvah, Yona the dove, beloved wife of Lotan, was mournful. At nights, she faithfully knelt down and prayed before going to sleep, and in the morning she awoke with another prayer on her lips. Throughout the day there was prayer in her heart, and she watched the babies and the children grow and become tough little descendants of the wilderness.

And another rainy season came, and another, and with the rains that wet her cheeks and her uplifted eyes, Yona wept for sadness and for fear. Of all of these women here, was she to be the only one who could not give her husband the gift of a son? Or a daughter—now *any* child would have seemed a gift of God to her. They did not need a son—only a little baby child for her to hold, for her to give suck to as the other mothers gave suck, to cuddle on these wet, dreary days, to rock to sleep when it cried.

The winter was long, and it was wet, and the fleas multiplied so thickly on the camels that they came in droves into the tents, and the people had to fight them constantly. Sometimes the boredom and the futility of it overcame them, and there were times when Yona would lie on her bed of robes, motionless, and watch the fleas that crawled back and forth, and bounced from one place to another. Was there no end to this? Was life one long procession of sadness, and rainy winters, furnace-like summers . . . and the itchy, sore bites of fleas?

Sometimes Yona would sit at the door of her tent and watch Lotan with the others, planting seeds, harvesting, hunting with his sling, and with his fine bow. Nephi had taught the others to make bows of their own, and now everyone, even Elnathan's men, carried more than a sword or a sling with them when they ventured into the hills.

At times, Bedouin not of Bahram's tribe had wandered near this place, and they appeared lean and hungry and ready to do battle for what Lehi's people possessed. But faced with the grim faces of the mighty warriors Nephi and Elnathan and all of the others, armed with the finest of handmade bows and quivers full of arrows, the Bedouin always moved on, and there was uneasy peace. If they did stop, it was only to water their camels and their people, and they were closely watched until they disappeared from sight.

These wandering Bedouin who now knew of Lehi's presence made this a dangerous place, but worse was the scarcity of game here, now that they had stayed so long. It was getting so Nephi and his hunters had to wander far from camp in search of ibex or oryx or the occasional herd of gazelles, and never did they see a feral goat anymore in these bitter, barren wastelands. Sometimes there were the onagers, the wild asses, but of these they had been commanded in Leviticus not to partake. And sometimes there were the ostriches as well, but these giant birds were wary and remained a long ways off. They were living in this camp now mostly on dried meat as they awaited the harvest season so that they would have something to plant in their next resting place, and something more to eat than only meat.

Ishmael, to his own surprise, was still among the living. He had never talked to Ra'ya of the pain in his chest, but she knew and understood, and for this reason Ishmael was never made to do any of the hard work about camp. He had grown old and very weak, and he seldom moved from his place by his tent. His face was drawn and gray, and most often he sat with one arm cradling the other, both of them drawn up tight to his chest, and grimacing with the pain he would never admit. His beard was untrimmed, now down to his mid-chest but thin and scraggly, and his eyes were sunken far back in his skull.

Ra'ya would come to him and put her arm around him and sing to him quietly, and his grandchildren who were old enough would sit on his lap when he felt good enough to cuddle them. He would give them his old smile, now with many of his teeth gone, and he would put his hands on their tender cheeks.

He would sing to them,

Little babies, come to me;
Traveling through eternity.
Each and every one of you
Warm my spirit through and through.
When I die I'll still be here,
Watching you throughout the years,
So you will know the way to roam,
And find me in my heavenly home.

And then his voice would grow weak, and Ra'ya would have to take the children away, and tears would wet her cheeks which she hid faithfully from Ishmael with a tender smile.

Often, Ishmael's daughters would sit with him and talk, and old Ishmael, he would only listen, because usually he was too weak to say much. Then he would fade off to sleep, his face still full of pain, and they would kiss his forehead and leave quietly.

And then, one morning, Ra'ya walked up to Lehi's fire, where her five daughters were preparing breakfast, and she faced Lehi, her face calm, her eyes swollen. She gave them a little, solemn smile.

"My Ishmael is gone," she said.

Chapter Fourteen

The Voice of the Lord

There was much wailing in this place which they named Nahom. The name derived from the word *naham*, meaning to console one-self. Ra'ya and all of her daughters and her daughters-in-law cut their hair and put on sackcloth, and then they sat in ashes, in Jew-ish custom, and cried out their hearts aloud. Because Ishmael was a wealthy man, had they been back in Jerusalem, professional mourners might have been hired to add to the overall noise of wailing so that the shade of Ishmael might hear and be satisfied that he was missed.

Most of the men who wore beards also cut them and their hair and donned sackcloth, that very roughly woven fabric of camel or goats' hair, prickly and uncomfortable in the extreme.

A dead body was considered ritually impure in the days of the ancient Israelites, and the heat was fierce, so there was no delay in interring Ishmael, and some of the family rent their clothing as a sign of their mourning. They laid Ishmael to rest in the earth of this valley which had given so much life, and over the top of his resting place they piled great stones that even the most ravenous of wolves could not roll away.

A day of mourning, then two, gave way, and in their wake the daughters of Ishmael began to complain bitterly against Lehi. For a while, even young Rachel, now mother of three, spoke out against her father-in-law and wondered how her father might have fared had they been allowed to remain behind in Jerusalem and to live the life of normal Hebrew people, where his life would have been one of ease, living with his wealth and with servants to do his bidding and to ease his tired bones by taking on his labors.

Rachel, for a time, did not seem to realize that in complaining against Lehi she was complaining against her husband—and against the Lord.

Lying back in the shadows far from his tent, Nephi listened the second night to the ranting of Ze'eva, who had returned to Ra'ya's fire rather than remain at Lehi's tent as a daughter-in-law was expected by custom to do. Tonight, more than ever, Ze'eva was matching up to her Hebrew name, which meant "female wolf."

"We have suffered too much here!" she said, and there was a strange growl in her throat, only partially from dryness, Nephi thought. "Lehi claims to be a great prophet, and he has led us out of the land of our inheritance, and what have we got from it? What but to wander aimlessly in this horrible wilderness of serpents and scorpions, and fleas, and marauders who wait only for a chance to come down and kill us and take what little we still have? We have suffered hunger and thirst, and heat and cold, and now the game is gone and we will die here of hunger. And for what? Because he had a dream telling him that Jerusalem would be destroyed!"

"It is not just Lehi," Shedrar reminded them, as he was always wont to do. "Nephi is as much at fault as the old man—maybe more. He is the one with the black powers. He is the one who convinced everyone that he could heal, that he could work miracles."

And there was no voice to defend Nephi's name.

Thus the talk went on until deep in the night, and after Nephi could take it no more he retired to his bed, and Rachel came in long after him, laying down their youngest child, Ethan, into a bed of camel skin, this from a camel that had died on their journey. The other children, Rebekah and Zur, had been asleep for a long time now, bedded down by Lehi and Sariah.

Unlike last night, Rachel snuggled up very close to her husband, and softly she began to weep. Concerned, he rolled over to face her in the dark, and he put out his hand to her face. It was wet with tears.

"What is wrong, Rachel?"

"I have sinned against you, my husband. I beg your forgiveness."

For a long time, he held her close, patting her back. Finally, when she stopped sobbing, he asked, "In what have you sinned against me?"

"I allowed my sisters to speak against you and Father Lehi. And there were times that I complained as well. But I do not believe this, Nephi. I have seen your heart, and I have seen the heart of Father Lehi. He loves us. He does not hate. And he has saved us from the fate of all Jerusalem. I was made sad by the death of my father, and I was weak."

"I understand what you have been through, Rachel. I could not say it did not make me sad to hear you speak against me, but I always knew your heart as you did mine. Be at peace, my wife."

And so for that night they slept in complete love for each other, in their own piece of heaven, and diamond stars filled the sky. The full and majestic moon was of silver, making them as rich as any family of Jerusalem.

But the next day became worse than the first, and when it became so bad in Ishmael's camp that even Ari'el and Ginath could take it no longer and returned, repentant, to their tents, Nephi grew fearful for what would become of their encampment. Laman and Lemuel had moved their tents early in the day over to Ishmael's campsite, and Ra'ya came to Nephi well after dark that night. She was trembling with fear.

Ra'ya slapped the outside of Nephi's tent and urgently whispered his name. He awoke with a start and came out of the covers, throwing open the tent door to face his mother-in-law. "Mother Ra'ya! What is it?"

"Nephi, I do not know how to tell you this, but I feel that I must. This night your brothers and my sons are drinking wine, and they are not themselves."

"What more, Ra'ya? There is more."

"Oh, Nephi!" Ra'ya fell against him, and she shuddered so hard that he thought her overcome with a sickness.

Holding her out away from him, Nephi tried better to see her in the dark, but he could make out hardly a feature of her face. "Why do you weep so, Mother? You must tell me."

"I have heard for myself that they plan to take your life, Nephi! Yours and Lehi's both. They say that you have done many things to deceive them into believing you are true prophets, and that all you have said of the angels ministering unto you, and the Lord speaking with you, are lies. They believe that you intend to lead them farther into a strange wilderness, away from all civilization, and there to rule over them and be their king."

"Who is with them, Ra'ya?" Nephi asked.

"They are the ones who talk, Nephi—Laman, Lemuel, and my own sons and three nephews. But there are others who listen, and they have made not their thoughts known."

"Who are these?"

"They are friends of Elnathan—Reuven... and No'ach."

Nephi was stunned. Zoram had told him about Reuven starting to lean toward his brothers' way of thinking. He had heard that he longed for his home in Jerusalem, and he wanted to go back there to his family. But this was the first time he had heard anything about No'ach the stone thrower consorting with his brothers and the sons of Ishmael.

He could not believe what he heard. For so long he had felt that he and No'ach were connected in many ways, that their friendship was growing as strong as any two friends could share. Even more than this grave word of his own brothers, hearing these things of No'ach made Nephi feel like he had been kicked in the stomach.

Nephi bent and kissed Ra'ya's cheek. "Mother Ra'ya, do they know where thou hast gone?"

"They do not. I told them I must make water."

Nephi smiled, familiar enough with Ra'ya to know that saying this would make her very uncomfortable. "Then you must return to your tent in silence, or if you wish, you may go to my father's tent, and sleep there tonight. For I fear what trouble this night might bring."

"Do not go there tonight, Nephi," she pled with him, squeezing his hands. "Tonight, with the wine speaking to them, they will try to kill you. Instead, you must go away. Flee from here and hide."

"Go to my father's tent, Ra'ya," Nephi now insisted, hardening his jaw. "It will be safe there."

"But—"

"Believe me, Mother. You will be safe."

After Ra'ya was gone, Nephi stepped back inside his tent and knelt beside Rachel. "They will try to kill us if something isn't done, my wife. I must go to them in the Lord."

"Please do not go, Nephi!" she pled. "Don't go."

But the will of Nephi was not to be put aside, and in his big, muscular arms she felt so safe and secure that she let him go, in the end, and then young Rachel lay staring up at the black ceiling of her tent, listening into the night—praying.

Outside the tent, Nephi knelt in prayer. He beseeched the Lord for safety and guidance, and these things he was promised. He felt a wave of strength come over him, and every part of him prickled with the sensations of the spirit as he came to his feet at last. Girding the sword, Elnathan, about his waist, along with the scimitar given him by Namir, he started off toward the tents of Ishmael.

The scene at Ishmael's camp was almost devilish. They had a fire going, a big fire, in spite of the danger of marauders, and in its light Laman and Lemuel, Shedrar, Hidai, Gera and Yavin were standing, brandishing their swords. The sword Laman held was the sword of Laban, whom Nephi had slain, and in the firelight it glowed and shimmered like a living thing. Nephi wondered if Laman even remembered his little brother had given it to him as a gift.

Joab and Reuven, Neriah, and Eran were still seated, and still imbibing of wine. But Nephi could not see No'ach. Suddenly, he felt his skin begin to crawl. Somewhere out in the dark was this deadly dangerous man who could hit a rabbit in the head with his sling at forty yards. For all Nephi knew, No'ach was behind him now. And how could he forget that upon their first encounter No'ach had almost slain him with a stone?

But then the Spirit of God surged up in Nephi again, and he knew he would be protected. With a mighty roar, he stepped into the edge of the firelight, his sword still sheathed.

"Ye demons from hell! Cease your words of war and murder. Cease conspiring in the dark."

His brothers and Shedrar whirled to face him, and Joab lunged up from his seat on the ground. Reuven also came upright, drawing his sword from its sheath. Neriah and Eran stood up, but rather than draw their swords they backed a few steps away.

Then suddenly Nephi heard a yell from behind him, and for one moment he feared death.

It was the voice of No'ach!

Time stood still. Nephi was bade of the Lord not to turn around, and he did not. But with all that was in him he expected a stone to strike him from No'ach's sling, and the thought flashed through his mind briefly, wondering how the Lord would protect him from that. No'ach... He could not believe that friend had turned against him.

Then Nephi heard the roar of Elnathan, and in a heartbeat they were standing beside him—Elnathan, Lehi, Ilai, Zoram, Sam, Lotan... and No'ach. The stone thrower had not turned at all! He had only gone for help. He was still Nephi's friend.

Before any man could move or react, there came a sound into the camp like the clap of thunder, and the mountains seemed to rumble with its mighty reverberation. Nephi's brothers cringed, as did the others with them, but the sound only emboldened Nephi, and he stood up straighter. His skin rose in chill bumps as a feeling of the spirit surged through his veins.

There was a moment of death-like stillness, a moment when if one listened one might hear the beating of a heart. And then, with a voice more mighty than a lion, words came to Ishmael's camp—from above them, from beneath them, from all around. And all within earshot of the camp knew they were listening to the voice of the Lord:

O, ye wicked and perverse men, ye who consort with the devil, who speak evil words in the dark, who contrive to lay low the righteous ways of the Lord for your own purposes! Laman, Lemuel, Reuven, and ye sons of Ishmael. Through your evil and excessive partaking of this wine, through your evil speaking of the anointed of the Lord, thou hast brought thyselves lower than the very dust at thy feet. When thy brother Nephi, and thy father Lehi have done nothing but seek me in righteousness, ye have fought to pervert their righteous ways. Ye have sought to turn their own people against them, and for this ye are cursed. Because ye are of the people of Lehi and of Ishmael, they who have been righteous in my sight, I spare thy lives this night. But be it known to ye that Nephi has been appointed as thy leader, and him shall ye follow all the days of thy lives, or thou shalt be condemned.

From this time forth, it is required of thee to follow thy father Lehi and thy brother Nephi in all that they ask of thee, and if thou wilt do this thing thou shalt be blessed with a promised land more bountiful than any land heretofore known to the covenant people of Israel.

As suddenly as the voice had come down, it went quiet, and a strange wind whirled across the camp and through the midst of the fire, scattering coals to every side and vanishing into the night.

Nephi's brothers and the sons of Ishmael and Reuven had all fallen to their knees on the ground, and some of them, including even Shedrar, wept. Lemuel wailed, "It was the wine, brother! It was not us talking. Please believe me. We would not truly have been able to hurt you or our father. You know this, do you not?"

Striding to Lemuel, Nephi had no thought of hurting him, or any of the others. He wanted only for them all to be at peace. But when he reached out a hand toward his brother, Lemuel cringed and crouched down as if expecting a blow.

"Lemuel," said Nephi, his voice deep and soothing. "Why do ye fear me, for I have never threatened to hurt you? Do not bow to me—I am only your brother." Lemuel opened his eyes, and when he saw Nephi holding out his hand to him he took it, and Nephi brought him to his feet.

Nephi then turned to Laman, but he was already coming up, his face stricken with a look of horror. Like the others, he gaped at Nephi but also looked all around, as if he expected lightning to come out of the sky and strike him down.

"Be at peace," Nephi said to all of them who had come to their feet and stood quaking before him. "I did not ask for the Lord to come. I came only to talk with you. But I see now that the Lord knew what had to be done. Praise be to the Lord God of Israel, for I know he has spared lives on this night."

Throughout the camp all was silence. Even the little children in their tents, whom Nephi had expected to be crying after the loud voice from on high, were silent, and now he wondered if any of them had even heard. Perhaps only those who had faced each other at the fire had heard the voice of the Lord, and the chastening of those who meant to do evil.

With tears staining his cheeks, Shedrar suddenly turned around and walked out of the firelight, his limbs shaky, and in moments he disappeared inside his tent, where Tikvah had been standing and waiting for him. Joab and his cousins slowly followed his example, going to their own tents, and Nephi, Laman and Lemuel stood together now with Reuven in the shadows.

Nephi saw Elnathan walk past him, hulking large in the shadows, and he walked to his comrade, Reuven, and stood in front of him. Nephi sensed that they each wanted to speak, but so powerful had been the experience for all of them that neither could, and no words passed between them, only looks.

Laman took a halting step forward and clutched Nephi's arm. "Once more I have been quieted, brother. And Lemuel was wrong: This wine is no excuse. I am sorry for what I have said. It is just..."

"I know you wish to be back in our home of comfort, Laman. In some ways I might wish that too. But the destruction of Jerusalem is nigh, and I could not lose you to that. And besides, you know that your life would be forfeit if you returned there. They will not forget the death of Laban. Even if we all wanted to return, we could not."

Laman bowed his head, and for a moment he could find no more words. Suddenly, he unloosed his belt from about his waist. His sheath and the sword of Laban were still hanging from it, and he dropped it on the ground at Nephi's feet. "Take back this sword of Laban, Nephi. I will never trust myself with it again."

"But it was a gift to thee, my brother," said Nephi, gazing into Laman's eyes.

"Take it back, Nephi, or I will cast it into the cavity of a rock where it will never more be found. The sword of Laban was meant to be thine, not mine."

And so, with a heavy heart, Nephi bent and picked up Laban's sword, and with a last look at his brother, a look of great sadness, he turned and walked away toward his tent.

Laman's humility tonight was fleeting, only while the fear of Yah-weh's visit was still strong in his memory. Nephi had lost all faith that his brother would ever change. This realization broke his heart.

Chapter Fifteen

Desperation

The next morning, very early, they heard the roar of a lion, and Nephi picked up his bow and ran outside to see to the stock. As he was nearing the outskirts of camp, he saw a herd of seven oryx running, exhausted, from a pride of lions. Sweat ran down their white flanks. All at the same time, Nephi saw the herd of oryx and the lions, the oryx and the lions saw Nephi, and all of them stopped. Leery, the lions turned broadside, and then so did the foremost oryx, a large, sleek female.

Suddenly, Nephi knew these lions were not here as a threat. They had come of the Lord only to bring Nephi's people food. Raising his bow, he brought down the oryx with one arrow. With complete unconcern, the lion pride then turned and padded away, and the other oryx trotted off, their big ears flapping back and forth, tails twitching, and their eyes rolling backward to make sure the lions were not still following.

And the people of Nephi did eat, and their stomachs were filled, and there was joy in the place called Nahom.

That night it was commanded of Lehi that they begin to harvest their grains. This work took only a week for the barley, then a week for the wheat, so great was their labor force now. The threshing, then the winnowing, was a time of laughter and celebration, singing and dancing, even in spite of the grain dusts and chaff which collected on their clothing and stuck to their sweaty skin beneath, tickling them, making them itch.

The last night in Nahom was again a night of peace and celebration, and in the dark of the night, forbidden by the Lord to make a fire, they bathed the grain dust from their weary bodies and prepared to travel on.

Early in the morning, the liahona directed them nearly eastward, completely away from the sea, and by its direction they made their new journey. Nephi and No'ach stood together, side by side, and looked out over the sea as the others began to trail away behind them, toward the east.

"I will miss this," said No'ach. "Somehow, these waters have come to be like a friend to me."

"I feel the same," said Nephi, clapping his friend on the shoulder. "It is hard for me to turn away from these blue waters."

"Do you think we will ever be here again?" asked No'ach. "I would hate to think my eyes would never more behold this beauty."

A flock of sea birds came overhead, their cries like the faint mewlings of a cat. Nephi drew a great breath and sighed. "My feeling is that we won't. I feel that we will never return in this direction. But ahead of us there are other wonderful things that wait as well. It is simply time for another adventure, new places we do not know."

There were tears in No'ach's eyes as he turned with Nephi away from the Red Sea, for the very last time.

From that time forth, they traveled eastward, and the desert face was fierce and full of fire.

No longer were they to smell the salt of the sea, no longer to feel any of the cool breezes which occasionally swept up off of the crystal blue waters. Before them now, they faced the greatest desert of sand on earth.

This was the Rub' al Khali.

The Rub' al Khali desert was known in other words as the Empty Quarter, or the quarter of emptiness, and in some places it was over six hundred miles across. Where the people of Lehi turned east, it was over five hundred.

From there on, in no place now did they take any long rests, nor did they sleep in shady places with good water for more than a few days' time before moving on again. There was a sense of urgency to their journey now, for to pause here long was to die, and the Lord's speech about the Promised Land, coupled with the forsaken desert around them, spurred them on.

In waking and sleeping dreams they could envision a place of waterfalls and of seashores, of tall, waving grass, fruit trees and grain, animals of all kinds, and birds and bees in the air. Of bee hives and honey, and climbing grape vines covered with purple fruit. These were the images that kept them moving, and from evenfall until midmorning, the only times they could travel now, they dreamed endlessly of it.

Here where pickings were slimmest, the danger of being attacked was greatest, and most times the Lord continued to bid them make no fire. So many times they ate raw meat, made sweet by the blessing of the Lord, feeling fortunate if they could at least dry it on top of the camels' packs as they traveled or as they rested of a day when the temperature topped one hundred twenty degrees in the shade.

Feet were cracked, and at times they bled, and this was the common state of their lips now as well—cracked and bleeding, and their tongues swollen and thick. Eyes were always bloodshot, for the Arabian sands seemed endless, and they sparkled, but it no longer resembled diamonds, only tiny bits of flame.

Yet somehow they slogged on through the hated red sand, and remembering the voice of the Lord that had come to their camp in Nahom kept them from complaining, kept their eyes always forward to that Promised Land that awaited them, somewhere.

They slogged over, and sometimes within, the shadows of red sand dunes that reared sometimes six hundred feet over their heads. The sand, torn and whipped and tortured by the wind, made all sorts of weird shapes that changed with each day and night. The sun baked them from above, and its rays shot off of the red and pink and orange sands and burned them from below. Nephi's three fine Arabian horses walked with heads bowed, padding forward obediently, knowing they had only to trust to their master to bring them to water. And their blind faith at times made him want to weep, for he could see they were fading.

Here in the Rub' al Khali, almost all wildlife had disappeared. There were insects, sometimes scorpions or spiders. Rarely, snakes or small rodents. Hardly a bush grew now, and seldom was there enough fuel to burn, even if the Lord had allowed it.

Water was rationed strictly, as was the dried meat. There were only seven goats and seven sheep left, a male and six females of each, which the Lord cautioned them to keep at all costs, for breeding purposes.

Now, all of the camels' humps were shriveled and shrunken down, as the water for these ships of the desert was held back sharply, and some of them had lost a full thirty percent of their body weight.

And amid all of the torment, the fire of the days and the ice of the nights, the sandstorms that sometimes over-swept them without warning, three more of the wives of Lehi's camp gave birth to children. In the wilderness in those endless-seeming years of travel were brought to earth thirty new little mouths to feed.

Out ahead of the others, little Montu son of Joab often rode beside Nephi. Montu was now in age ten years old, and he was larger than a boy of his age should be and muscular beyond reckoning. He rode beside Nephi, and always he observed his uncle's skills in tracking, in hunting, in nature lore. But never did Montu smile, and seldom did he even speak. Once, Montu had been stung by a large black scorpion, and through the following four days of chills and fever he had sweated and he had shaken and gritted his teeth. But Montu, named for the Egyptian god of war, never cried.

Yo'ash son of Shedrar could not match his cousin, for he would cry if Ari the camel gave out a roar too near his tender ears. Behind his back and that of his father the boy was the laughing stock of the men of the camp, all of them except Nephi, who had a tender heart for little Yo'ash.

Perhaps even more so, Nephi had a tender spot for four other children not his own. These were the children of his good friend Elnathan: Barak, Little Nephi, Little Rachel, and a third son, an infant, they named Little Lehi.

The little ones were growing up alongside Nephi's own children, Rebekah, Zur and Ethan, and it made Nephi's heart swell in the evenings at camp to watch them play together. Zur, his oldest son, had been named that, meaning "big rock," because from his very birth he was such a large child. And the boy showed no signs of stopping. But from a very tender age it was Ethan, two years Zur's younger, who showed sign of great intelligence, and even as a one-year-old seemed to be so wisely pondering every move before he made it. Nephi thought Zur and Ethan would make a great pair if they could always stay friends.

Then one night, a night when they found a well with water in it, a voice whispered to Lehi that it would be all right for them to make a fire, and the people rejoiced because of it and the larger portions of water they received.

Beside the fire they laughed and danced, and those who knew how played music. Sariah, even with her fingers cracked and bleeding, played the lute, and never had it sounded more beautiful and luring. The daughters of Ishmael sang, and even Tikvah, although she had always been ashamed of her voice, joined in.

Lehi sat smiling at these people, *his* people, and his heart felt good. Nephi came and sat down next to him, and Lehi put his hand over that of his son. "I am very proud of you, Nephi. You have been all that a father could ask for. Even at times when I gave in to weakness you did not murmur. For this you will be blessed, and in time you will be the leader of a mighty people."

"I do not ask for this, Father. I ask only for peace among my family."

Lehi gave him a smile, patting his hand. "Not always can we have those things which we desire most, my son. Some of us come into this world for another purpose than mere peace, and from the Lord I know this is the case for you.

"Some are born to greater things than their childhood can foretell, and yet you, Nephi, were not one of these. From a young age I knew you would be a leader—not just a leader of your own family, but of many families—a leader of nations. We will soon reach our promised land, Nephi. This I feel tonight in my heart. You have won this, and you deserve to reap the rewards. Always look forward, my son, and never forget the Lord, who has given you all that you have."

Lehi stood up abruptly, and he took a skin full of wine that he had made—new wine, with no alcohol content in it. "We cannot see it yet, my people, but we will soon reach the promised land, a land more beautiful than anything we have yet beheld, even in the land of Jerusalem. Let us drink tonight to the promised land."

But even in the cool dark, his people thought of the sand that lay behind them and of all the endless dunes they had stared at before them, and it was hard to believe.

Yona and Lotan sat together and watched the dancing, watched the firelight play on the golden harp, and listened to the voices singing. Children played, and all was beautiful, but Yona's eyes shone with tears.

There were many new children in this camp, and some of those who had wed the same day as she now had four, while Yona had none. Many nights she had wept for her barrenness, and she had prayed, and her prayers seemed unanswered. Tonight, she found her eyes on Nephi, and something told her to go to him, and beg him for his help.

So, suddenly standing, she reached down and took Lotan's hand, and he arose with her, and she led him over to Nephi.

Nephi smiled at the couple when they stopped, and he quickly jumped up. "Shalom, my friends."

"Shalom," they replied. And Yona said, "Nephi, I would like to speak with you for a moment."

So Nephi led them away into the shadows between the camp and the camels, and he turned with his back to the fire, just able to see the details of Yona's and Lotan's faces, though because of the fire behind him they could not see his. "What is it, Yona?"

Yona now seemed loath to speak, and she looked down, fidgeting with her fingers.

"Tell me, Yona—why are you troubled?"

"For many years I have prayed that we might have a child. I have prayed, Nephi, and nothing has happened. I have not been able to give Lotan a child when all around me babies are being born."

"Yes," said Nephi.

Yona looked up at him quickly, searching his eyes. "Yes?"

"Yes, I will bless you, Yona. And if you have the faith then you shall receive what you ask of the Lord."

"But I had not asked you," she said, stunned. "How did you know?"

"The Lord hath spoken, Yona."

So Nephi called his father and Sam to him, and together they laid hands on Yona's head, and Nephi spoke the words of blessing that came to him. They were words that he could not speak himself, but words he had prayed for, for many years he and Rachel had watched Yona and had mourned for her barrenness. He had been waiting only for the young woman to come to him in faith and ask.

"Yona, by your faith in the Lord God of Israel, you will be blessed with a child, a child bright and strong, who one day will become a leader of many people and whose offspring will one day accomplish mighty and wonderful feats." Tears flooded Nephi's eyes, and his voice broke so that he almost could not finish the blessing, and Yona looked up at him, crying, and Lotan was crying too.

"I believe, Nephi. I believe in you," Lotan said.

Nephi smiled, sniffling. "Believe not in me, my friend. Believe in the Lord."

The next four days were hell. Across the endless wastes they plodded, and the sand dragged them down, seemed to suck at their feet as if they were walking in water—yet there was no water. Here, the sand was soft and fine, and it made for very laborious walking.

They would cease to walk in midmorning, when the sun battered them mercilessly, and they would set up a pavilion, under which they would crawl and sleep the sleep of the dead. Even the camels seemed to be dying, and they bunched close together, because this was how camels cooled themselves, by feeding off the cooler air that came off of their own bodies, as only a camel's body will do.

Because the water supply had been so meager even at their last camp, the camels had been allowed to drink but little, and there were several that seemed on the verge of death. Sadly, old Abraham was one of these.

The big camel, "father of many," had seen good years, but now he was growing old. Nephi sat beside him and stroked his neck, chasing fleas out of his hide. Abraham grunted and closed his eyes, liking the feel of Nephi's fingernails against his skin.

All around them stretched the red dunes, and overhead there was no cloud in the bronze sky. Most of the people were sleeping now, even with the sweat trickling into their eyes. Some had their eyes open, and they stared dully, like mummies, like bodies meant for the grave.

One more day. Perhaps two. They could make it no more. Nephi said a silent prayer as he held Rachel to him and looked at his baby boy. People were going to die if they did not reach water soon, for what was left in the goat skins was almost nothing.

The fine Arabian horses, however, would go first, for they could no longer afford water for them, and they had gone two full days without. Fingering the dangling necklace about his neck, looking down at the big red piece of coral, Nephi thought sadly of Bahram, the sheikh. He would be sad if he could see his fine horses now. He looked at the ring, and absently spun it around his finger, which like the rest of him had shrunk to the point of gauntness. Too long had they gone now without proper nourishment. Even Nephi, he of the great stature, had little strength left.

Late that evening, almost upon an unspoken command, the people began to rouse, and moving very slowly and mechanically they stood and readied themselves and their animals. Nephi noticed all of a sudden that one of his father's dogs was lying dead on the sand. It was ten years old, and the strain of the heat and lack of water and food had been too much. Another got up, its head hung low and tongue lolling out, and it looked about blankly, asking for nothing, expecting less.

Nephi went to Lehi before everyone began to mount. "Father, should I ride ahead and try to find water? I could try to bring some back."

Lehi gave his son a sympathetic smile. "My son, it would do no good now. You could as easily die out there alone, far from your family."

Laman had walked close, and he looked from Lehi to Nephi. "I feel that this is our last day," he said.

Lehi looked at him, surprised. "You feel that we are near the end of our travels, my son? That is good!"

"No, father," said Laman wearily. "Not in a good way. This night some of us will die. My little Ruth is already near to death, and she will not make it far."

Lehi's face fell, and he went to Laman's daughter. The girl's face was bright red, but she was no longer sweating. Lehi washed her face with cool water, and she stared up at him as if he did not exist. "Night is falling, my child. You will be safe."

He and Nephi, and even Laman, laid their hands upon the child, and Lehi offered words of blessing. Ruth stirred, and she tried to smile. When Laman climbed onto his camel, Nephi placed the girl in his brother's arms, and then the camel rose up to its full heigh, on shaky legs. Laman carried Ruth with him as the sun sank into the broad, ruddy dunes and night swept over them, and a cool wind began to blow.

In the night, they traveled for over twenty miles, Lehi reckoned, and the camels walked with their heads down. Sometimes one of them would stumble, and once Abraham fell to his knees. Nephi obligingly dismounted and walked beside him, for now they could travel no more than three miles an hour, and Nephi's long legs, even in his state of dehydration and in the deep sand, could manage that speed.

The stars overhead were dancing, and the tarnished silver moon beamed bright on the waves of sand. It was like an endless, unforgiving ocean. Other people than Nephi were off their camels and walking, and some of them who were still mounted slept, and their heads bobbed fiercely up and down. Even some of the camels seemed to sleep, and they plodded endlessly on and on and on.

Lotan walked up on Nephi and tried to say something, but his voice would make no sound. In his mouth his tongue was too swollen to work. He smiled through cracked lips, then satisfied himself by simply patting Nephi's arm. Nephi nodded his understanding. He did not even try to speak.

Nephi wanted to walk back along the line of people, to see how they all fared. But he did not dare. All of their water was gone now, and there was no longer anything he could do for any of them. If any were dying, the Lord must take them this night or on the morrow. He wondered how far they must go, and for the first time he found himself wondering how many would make it.

It was very early in the morning, and the moon had descended far down the sky. It was very dim now against the gray light in the sky. In that single night they had forced themselves on and had traveled over twenty miles–not a long distance for a caravan to travel, but very long for camels and people who were dying of thirst. There was no sound of voice from anyone, man or beast.

But for no apparent reason the camels suddenly began to fight their reins, and soon some of them started into a clumsy lope, and their riders let them go. The horses, too, perked up their heads and began almost to prance forward, or at least what had to pass for a prance in this state of dehydration. Nephi had seen this behavior in the animals a few times before, and always it had meant water ahead.

A strange scent came into the air, and it was not a smell of the desert, but of trees, and grass, and greenery. They soon came within sight of what appeared to be a forest of trees, their bold silhouettes ragged against the morning sky. They rushed on, forgetting how tired they were, and in time they entered the most lush of all the oases they had stayed in during their eight years of travel, even more fruitful and beautiful than the Valley of Lemuel. Palm trees bowed over a large pool of water with three different springs spilling into it and grass bending over its banks. Other trees stood back from the water, stately and serene, whispering in the breezes of the dawn. Early-waking birds trilled in the trees, and a herd of some large animals, possibly gazelles, stampeded and fled from the vicinity and disappeared into the blackness of trees beyond.

Nephi walked with Abraham to the water, and when he knelt and tasted of it trickling out of one of the springs it was the clearest, the coolest water he had tasted in years. He called the others to him, and it was all the riders could do to keep their camels back from the water's edge while the people slaked their thirst. Nephi took special care to make sure the horses only had a small amount of water before tying them up to trees not far off. He would let the water settle in them for a time, then let them drink again.

There were vast areas here where tents could be pitched, but to the surprise of all Lehi said, "We will not be staying here long. Let us not pitch our tents."

This command did not bother anyone, for so serene was the weather, and so long and weary had been their travel that endless night that they had not relished the thought of putting up all the huge tents in the dark anyway. This wonderful early morning, they all sank down underneath the few stars that battled on, and the heavens had never seemed brighter. There was a freshness to the air they had not smelled in many months, and the grunting of the camels while they munched on the lush grasses was a sound of deep comfort.

The rising sun was not far off, but already Nephi could hear the peaceful breathing all around him of his family and friends, who had already drifted off into peaceful sleep.

It was not fifteen minutes later when a voice seemed to call to Nephi, and he opened his eyes and looked around him. The sky in the east, the direction of their travel, was turning purple-pink on the horizon, and silhouetted there was the shape of a man... Lehi.

Nephi managed to push up to his feet and went to his father, and they stood side by side looking at the gathering light in the east. Gold began to filter up into the sky, and soon became a light that put to shame all of the worldly riches Lehi and his family had ever possessed.

From a ways away, Nephi heard grass rustling, and he looked over to see his good friends Zoram and Elnathan approaching. "I do not know what has awakened me," said Zoram, "but I am glad it did. I have never beheld such a sunrise."

"Nor have I," agreed Elnathan.

Nephi smiled and slapped his friends on the back. "I am glad you are here, my friends. It is right that we should see this together."

In another moment, he heard footsteps come up behind him, and he found his Rachel ducking under his arm. Lehi and Zoram looked over and smiled at them both.

"Let us walk together, my children," said Lehi.

Lehi started out, his steps long and steady, never wavering from side to side. The golden light continued to grow until it swept over most of the eastern sky, far to either side, and so high up overhead that they could not see it all at one glance.

It was as an immense, sparkling sheet of gold spread with the brush of God over a ceiling of pink and purple and orange linen cloud, a light of gold almost blinding in its boldness.

And then, not a quarter of a mile from where they had started out, they began to see tree tops, dozens of them—*dozens* of dozens, and bird calls of every kind filled the morning. The black silhouettes of a flight of pelicans swept by, and their wings were so great that their beats could be heard even from forty feet below, and they were headed into the blazing sunrise.

Then the mountainside swept off before them, dense black with foliage, and all along in front of them and to either side was a vast tract of forest, and stretched out before them to the horizon a tremendous body of water mimicked the gold of the sky over-head, and in the distance great waves could be heard lapping at the shores that ran on and on to either side. Strange bird calls filled the air, the like of which none of them had ever heard, and the dew-covered grasses brushed their legs and drenched their san-daled feet.

And Lehi and his children wept at the beauty of it, for they had never in all of their days beheld a sight more beautiful.

"Could this be our promised land?" asked Zoram, the first one to find his voice.

Nephi beheld the beauty of this place, smelled of the freshness of its air, tasted the salty wind on his tongue, and although it was beautiful and serene and seemed beyond idyllic, a quiet whisper-ing in his spirit told him it was not yet enough.

He wanted this to be it. He wanted to rest here forever. But this place, from what he could behold, was not the wonderful place he somehow knew awaited them.

The journey to their final land of promise had only begun.

EPILOG

For eighteen long and weary months the mighty Jerusalem was under siege, and within his opulent vermilion palace, the palace built up by his wicked brother Jehoiakim on the backs of slave labor, young King Zedekiah, now thirty-two years of age, cowered and prayed. But his prayers were too weak... and too late.

The food within the city was mostly gone, and for some of the people, those called the "people of the land," who were already poor when the siege began, their food had been gone for some time, and in utter desperation they had even resorted to eating straw, and dung—and even of their own dead.

Zedekiah had believed on the words of Jeremiah, upon his prophecies of Jerusalem's destruction, but unlike his righteous father, Josiah, he had proven unable to go up against the city elders, who were so adamant against Jeremiah that more than once they had insisted on Zedekiah casting him into a dungeon, since in Jerusalem they did not have an actual prison for criminals. In that dungeon Jeremiah would have died had not others come to beg Zedekiah for his life and had not Zedekiah secretly allowed him to be removed from the pit and secreted in the palace.

Some of the city elders, or princes, had come to Zedekiah prior to the siege and asked him to have Jeremiah put to death. These men were Shephatiah the son of Mattan, Gedaliah the son of Pashur, Jucal the son of Shelemiah, and Pashur the son of Malchiah. In their words to Zedekiah, Jeremiah, with his dire prophecies, was weakening the hands of the men of war who remained in the city.

And although Zedekiah hated, even scorned himself for it, he knew he did not have the strength of his father, King Josiah, and he told the princes it was in their hands, and that he was unable to do anything against them. This by now was already known to all.

So the princes took Jeremiah and cast him into a dungeon of Malchiah the son of Hammelech that was in the court of the prison. This dungeon was no more than a cistern, but the water in it was gone, and now it was merely mire, refuse, and dung.

Eventually, one of the eunuchs had come to Zedekiah pleading to have Jeremiah drawn up out of the dungeon, where he would surely die, and this Zedekiah agreed to, in secret.

He brought Jeremiah before him and asked him if he had spoken with the Lord, and Jeremiah's word was affirmative. Zedekiah swore to Jeremiah that if he would tell him the truth he would not allow him to be killed, and Jeremiah agreed. Once again, he told Zedekiah that if he would go to Nebuchadnezzar he would be preserved, that he needed only to surrender.

But this Zedekiah could not bring himself to do, for fear that once he was carried away to Babylon he would be turned over to the Jews who were already there, and they would beat him and otherwise mistreat him. And so Zedekiah kept Jeremiah safe and secure and well fed in the court of the prison, and he waited...

And now none of this mattered any longer. The words of Jeremiah had come to pass, as Zedekiah had feared—yea, every whit. Zedekiah had cowed to the city elders, and because of this he was perceived by Nebuchadnezzar as a rebel. In the ninth year of Zedekiah's reign as king, in the tenth month, Nebuchadnezzar came up against Jerusalem, and no aid was forthcoming from the pharaoh in Egypt, the one place Jerusalem had looked for relief.

Outside of the city, Nebuchadnezzar's army built siege walls, and they brought up machines of war, battering rams. They blocked off all routes into and from the city, then settled in to wait.

The months inched by, and for a time the people of Jerusalem continued to believe that the Lord would yet deliver them. They were, after all, the children of the promise. The Lord would preserve them and his temple, the wonderful temple of Solomon.

But the siege continued, and the food and the water dwindled. Sickness came upon Jerusalem when the wine began to run out and the people were forced to drink the diseased water from the cisterns beneath the city.

Pestilence swept the population, and with it famine. The olives disappeared, and the cakes of dates and figs, and the dried fish and meat. Soon, all of the grain became scarce, even the barley, the grain of the poor man, and the people grew gaunt, and the children and the women, and even some of the men wept in the streets, where many lay dying.

The priests and the false prophets began, too late, to turn from their evil ways, but Zedekiah did not perceive that this change of heart was real. It was only out of fear. And Jeremiah remained in the palace, hidden, and from time to time Zedekiah went to him. But the time when he could have acted was gone. Zedekiah's time as ruler was drawing short.

The stench of the dead and dying lay like a pall over the beautiful city, and the people ate all of the animals, down to the last dog, and they ravenously trapped and ate the rats that came up out of their holes and tried to scavenge for food among the houses.

And, in ultimate desperation, sometimes when a child would die, its own parents would eat of its flesh as the last days drew near, and the children ate the flesh of their parents, and the brothers of their brothers.

And at last, in the eleventh year of Zedekiah's reign, in the fourth month, on the ninth day of the month, when the days were most desperate, and when the Jews fought amongst themselves like ravenous beasts, all the princes of the king of Babylon came up and sat in the middle gate of the city, the Valley Gate. These men were Nergal-sharezer, Samgar-nebo, Sarsechim, Rab-Saris, and Rab-mag, with all the lesser of the princes of Babylon.

When this word came to Zedekiah, and when he was led there and shown this sight, and all the men and the machines of war of Babylon, he lost all hope, and he prayed to a God he had nearly forgotten and wished that he had followed his instincts, that he had been a braver man, and that he had made his kingdom to follow the words of Jeremiah and of Lehi.

In the night, he took all of his army, and his princes, and his sons, and he fled the dying city by the way of the king's garden, by the gate between the two walls, and in desperation he went out the way of the plain.

But the spies of the Chaldeans saw him depart, and the army pursued, and they caught up in the plains of Jericho. As the Chaldeans fell upon Zedekiah, his army fled him, scattering to the winds.

The Chaldeans easily captured Zedekiah, his princes and his sons, and they brought them to Nebuchadnezzar, who was in Riblah, in the land of Hamath. In Riblah, Nebuchadnezzar gave judgment upon them, and he slew all of the nobles who had fallen to him, and then with Zedekiah bound in chains and forced to watch he killed all of his sons—all, that is, but one—before his eyes.

The sole progeny of Zedekiah to escape, a young man of only twelve years of age, made his way with a group of protectors, friends of his father's, into the wastelands toward Egypt. The young man's name was Mulek, and he, like Nephi, had found favor with God.

As for his hapless father, Zedekiah, when the rest of his sons were gone, dead at his feet, and he knew not the whereabouts of young Mulek and feared the worst for him as well, Nebuchadnezzar had him brought to his knees, and with a hot iron from the fire he put out his eyes, to the sound of Zedekiah's screams.

Zedekiah, bound in his chains, was taken away to Babylon to live out his days, for Jeremiah had told him that he would not die violently, but that he would die in Babylon, in peace. For the rest of his days, Zedekiah would mourn the loss of his family, and he would wonder until his dying day what had become of Mulek, and those brave men and their women who had secreted him out and away from the city.

One month after capturing Zedekiah and his entourage, the captain of the Babylonian guard, one Nebuzar-adan, returned to the city, and his soldiers broke through the gates into the city. With wild abandon, the Chaldean soldiers swept through the city, on horseback and on foot, slaying with the sword, and with the bow and the arrow, the mace and the lance and the axe, every person of Jerusalem. By their weapons fell the old men, the crippled, the children, and the women. And they set on fire the palace of the king and all of the houses of the people, and they burned down the temple of Solomon after ransacking it and taking from it everything of value, and breaking down all the pieces of gold, and of silver, and of bronze, to carry away to Babylon.

Of the many poor people who were left, the Babylonians took captives, to carry them away to Babylon, but of the poorest of the land, who had nothing, Nebuzar-adan gave lands and vineyards, leaving them there as stewards.

And by the order of Nebuchadnezzar, he had Nebuzar-adan bring forth Jeremiah out of captivity. And to him was given the choice, because the king of Babylon knew that Jeremiah had been faithful and had always spoken in behalf of Babylon, whether to live in prosperity in Babylon or to stay in the land of Judah as a free man. Jeremiah chose to stay in Judah with those who were left in charge there, who numbered but few.

And thus, only ten years after Lehi had seen the fall of Jerusalem, the great city was sacked and burned, and most of its people killed or carried away, and the land of Judah left desolate. In time, the fortified cities of Lachish and of Azekah, south of Jerusalem, also fell, the last strongholds of the land of Judah, and their beacon lights vanished like stars fallen from the heavens.

And Nebuchadnezzar, king of Babylon, ruled all of the land. And the promise of the Lord God of Israel was fulfilled.

And for the once mighty Jerusalem the angels wept.

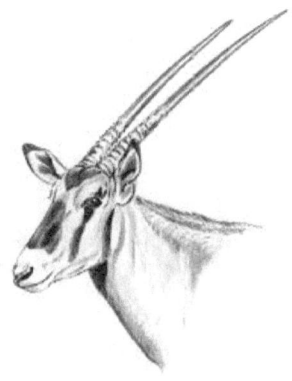

Next, look for:

LEHI'S DREAM, Book Four:
SHORES OF PROMISE

Chapter Notes

CHAPTERS TWO AND THREE: I used lions extensively in this part of the book for three reasons: one, to give Laman another reason to despise Nephi, who in his eyes indirectly caused the death of his Naomi by "making" him leave Jerusalem; two, to fulfill part of Nephi's words about "trials and tribulation," where the details were left mostly to the reader's imagination; and three, because I have always been fascinated by and a student of big cats and will take advantage of any chance I can to put them in my stories. There. I admitted it.

CHAPTERS FIVE AND SIX: I believe in my heart that there was much left out of the *Book of Mormon* in speaking of Laman and Lemuel that could have led the reader to a much deeper understanding of why they did the things they did. Most brothers who have grown up in normal, loving families do not easily choose to leave each other bound out in the middle of the fiery desert to be eaten by wild animals. With this belief in mind I have spent much time building up Laman and Lemuel's anger toward Nephi, and now we come back into events that are actual and recorded, such as this rebellion by Laman, Lemuel, and the sons of Ishmael.

Also factual is Nephi's prayer for deliverance and the subsequent falling away of the bands used to tie him up. I was able to use much that was fact in this section, as there are parts here where

Nephi has filled in a lot of detail for us. Although he did not say Rachel specifically, he did say that one of Ishmael's daughters and his wife and one son stood up for him, so I only had to choose which ones.

Following this incident, Laman, Lemuel, and others did indeed bow down to Nephi and beg his forgiveness, and Nephi forgave them and suggested that they pray.

CHAPTER SEVEN: Lehi's dream! I was relieved to be able to go into a section of the *Book of Mormon* where I had a real, full outline to follow, and I tried to stick as closely as I could to Nephi's words in relating Lehi's famous dream.

CHAPTERS EIGHT AND NINE: Again, I was given a full plate of factual story to follow in this chapter, and I pray that after reading it my readers will go back once again and study Nephi's actual words in describing his own dream, for they are most moving. I go from Nephi's vision into his meeting with Laman and Lemuel, which, once again, is one of the places where I only had to fill detail in to flesh out a factual account. The translation of the dream is mostly straight out of the *Book of Mormon* as well, including, as in other parts of this book, direct scriptural quotes.

CHAPTER TEN: As readers of the *Book of Mormon*, we already know that the four sons of Lehi married four of the daughters of Ishmael and that Zoram married the other. In this chapter I had the delight of filling in the details of an ancient Hebrew wedding ceremony and the feasting and celebration which surrounded it. Much of this ceremony, needless to say, could not possibly have been as it would have been if they had remained in Jerusalem, and I tried to make both the ceremony and what preceded it as believable and authentic as possible. I probably don't need to point out that Lotan and Yona's and Elnathan and Yael's weddings were only of my imagination, since of these characters Elnathan is the only one who actually existed, and he most likely was back in Jerusalem.

CHAPTER ELEVEN: Nephi was kind to me as a writer of fiction in giving me so much fact to build upon in this chapter speaking of their departure from the Valley of Lemuel. First, Lehi dreamed that it was time to leave, and then he found a "ball of curious workmanship," later in the *Book of Mormon* referred to as a "liahona," which I have been told in Hebrew means compass.

They then sally forth into the place they call Shazer, where they stay for a time slaying game. At some point, they travel on, and soon Nephi's bow breaks and his brothers' bows "lose their springs," leaving them without hunting implements. The majority of this is factual. I even had my good friend Trevor Valenzuela to tell me what happens when a bow breaks at full-draw. He actually took a pretty good punch to the face in his accidental but well-timed research on my behalf.

As to the bows losing their springs, an old-style hand-made wooden bow must be kept well-oiled and clean, and most especially in a place like that desert, where as strange as it may seem I have been told it often grows very humid, particularly along the mountain ranges such as where they were traveling at this point. There is speculation, and one cannot disagree, that this humidity might have been the cause of those "lost springs" in Laman, Lemuel, and presumably Sam's bows.

CHAPTERS TWELVE AND THIRTEEN: It is in this first chapter that we see the only disturbing moments when Lehi actually loses faith and begins to murmur about their hardships. Yet Nephi does not falter. He makes a bow and one arrow, and after bringing Lehi back to his faith, he follows his directions into the mountains, where he is able to kill game. All of this is factual and fantastic fodder for a fiction writer like me to fill in with detail as far as the actual game brought down, etc.

I mentioned the birth of Nephi's brother Jacob here, which he only mentioned later in the *Book of Mormon,* as an afterthought. All of the other births until that of Joseph, the last child of Sariah, are fictional, but we know that many children must have been born out there for them to have been able to populate their "Promised Land."

Sadly, in the camp called Nahom, Ishmael at last succumbed to his illness. In reality, there is no indication whatever of whether or not he was sick prior to this time or if his death was sudden and unexpected. I simply wanted to build this up so it didn't come upon the unfamiliar reader "out of the blue," so to speak.

CHAPTER FOURTEEN: Most of this chapter is fact, and I had only to fill in details of conversation, etc. The daughters of Ishmael began to murmur, and I assume that included Nephi's Rachel, as he did not say otherwise.

Laman, Lemuel, and the sons of Ishmael then got to the point in their anger where they decided at last to take the lives of Lehi and Nephi. But before they could follow through with their plans, the voice of the Lord came down and chastised them, and once more they repented. As there was very little detail given of this occasion, I was able to call heavily upon my literary license once more, but the basis of all of this was fact. It seems that it would have taken a very earth-shaking experience to get the likes of someone to apologize and repent who had decided to kill their own father and brother.

I chose this section as a cut-off place where Nephi at last realized his brothers were probably never going to change. Remember, they had seen an angel, seen Nephi released from his bonds, and now heard the voice of the Lord, but it would seem that if the angel didn't shake them up permanently nothing would. And Nephi had seen plenty of them by now, as well as other people, besides being a man given much wisdom by God. I believe he would have lost any of his earlier naivety.

CHAPTER FIFTEEN: It is here, at last, that the party of Lehi turns due east, and it is here that they start across the Empty Quarter—the Rub' al Khali, which is literally the largest desert of sand in the world. The Sahara, of course, is larger, but not comprised so much of sand as the Rub' al Khali. It is said that it is much fiercer in our modern day than it was then, but be that as it may, it was still a place that had to be very harsh and forbidding, even worse than the land of Midian they had already passed through, which Moses himself described in very unfavorable terms.

Of this part of the trip, Nephi gives us only the "much affliction" comment, so I had to rely on my research of this vast desert to fill in these blanks. All we know is that they suffered much, that the women bore children, that they ate their meat raw but that it was made sweet by the Lord. The rest of this section is from my imagination.

At last, they reached the Arabian Sea, in all likelihood in the famed frankincense country that in modern times is known as the country of Oman, where the book ends.

EPILOG: Surprisingly, I found little vivid detail on the final destruction of Zedekiah's Jerusalem. I found tidbits here and there, but as much in *The Bible* as anywhere else. However, most of what I portrayed, including the eating of dung and of one's own dead kin, is recorded history. King Zedekiah's capture, the killing of his sons and his court officers before him, and then his blinding with a hot poker, is all factual. Also accurate is the account of the slipping away of the one son, Mulek, of whom we will read again later in the series. Jerusalem came to its end, and its end, like its last eleven years, was very ugly, exactly as Urijah, Jeremiah, Lehi and Nephi had predicted it would be.

About the Author

Kirby Frank Jonas was born in 1965 in Bozeman, Montana and raised there in the heart of the "Wild West" until the age of five. Growing up with a brother and a father who loved the lore of the Old West, in a time when Western movies, television series, and toys were highly popular, it was only natural that Jonas, who grew into his lifelong love of art at the early age of two, would become an artist depicting the West.

His first work that could remotely be called fiction (other than, perhaps, the fibs of a boy with a big imagination) he wrote when he was six, in the style of comic books—a Western story with the plagiarized name of Joe Mannix for his main character.

When he was five years old, Jonas's family went on a forced march out to the state of Virginia, where his father taught school and worked at the Smithsonian Institute while he tried to finish his doctoral thesis in botany. Living on a remote farm in the middle of Civil War country near Broad Run, Jonas was the lucky child, for here he got to live the idyllic existence of a farm boy, but without all the chores. Their property in Virginia came complete with horses, a huge two story barn, a fish pond full of bass, bluegills, turtles and tadpoles, with banks teeming with bullfrogs and wild strawberries, and a creek swimming with trout.

Luckily, little boys are uprooted easily, so he didn't think much about what he was losing when they moved back out west to Shelley, Idaho, where Jonas was lucky enough to start school

and go all the way through in the same school system until grad-
uating in 1983. By then, he had a lifetime of Western dreams already under his belt, along with two completed Western novels
and a dozen more on their way.

Jonas ceased his budding writing career to serve an LDS mission in the France-Paris mission, serving there in six cities,
namely, Rennes, Tours, Le Havre, Caen, LeMans and Bordeaux,
much of this country in the very heart of World War II battle
lands.

Upon arriving back home, Jonas's sense of adventure had just
begun to bloom, and after seeing a whole new part of the world to
add to some thirty states he had already visited, he moved to
Mesa, Arizona, with plans of making a six-month horse pack trip
from the Mexican border to Cardston, Canada. Like many wonderful dreams, this one had to be put on hold, but while in Arizona
he worked as a security guard, and as the driver of an armored
truck for Wells Fargo (not a far cry from a stagecoach driver out
of the Old West!) and completed his in-depth research for his first
three novels, along with his seventh and part of his eighth.

Once back in Idaho, the home he had grown up with, Jonas
"finished" school, which was the only two semesters of "higher
education" he could stomach, then became a wildland firefighter
for the Bureau of Land Management for three years, worked for
the Idaho Fish and Game, and finally hired on as a police officer
for the City of Pocatello. He made a change to the Pocatello Fire
Department in 1993 and has been employed there ever since. In
2011, Jonas was awarded the coveted "Spur Award" from Western Writers of America for the best novel on audio, his *The Secret
of Two Hawks.*

Jonas has played the cowboy throughout all of his childhood,
and worked off and on as a cowboy for part of his adulthood, so
naturally the first eleven of his novels were Westerns. He has

since completed a semi-autobiographical novel taking place in Shelley in 1977, and has now begun this most ambitious undertaking of his writing career and probably his life: the series, *Lehi's Dream*.

Jonas is married to Debbie. They live in Pocatello and have four children, Cheyenne, Jacob, Clay and Matthew, two of whom, Clay and Matthew, have already had their own novels featuring them as the hero, and the other two who one day will.

Books by Kirby Jonas

Season of the Vigilante Book I (1994)
Season of the Vigilante Book II (1996)
The Dansing Star (1997)
Death of an Eagle (1998)
Legend of the Tumbleweed (1999)
Lady Winchester (2000)
The Devil's Blood (2001) (Combination of *Season of the Vigilante Book I/Book II)*
Yaqui Gold (2003) (co-author Clint "Cheyenne" Walker)
The Secret of Two Hawks (2012)
Samuel's Angel (2015)
Knight of the Ribbons (2013)
Drygulch to Destiny (2014)
The Night of My Hanging (and other stories) (2015)

LEGENDS WEST SERIES
Disciples of the Wind (2005) (co-author Jamie Jonas)
Reapers of the Wind (2006) (co-author Jamie Jonas)

LEHI'S DREAM SERIES
Nephi Was My Friend (2015)
The Faith of a Man (2015)
A Land Called Bountiful (2015)
Shores of Promise (forthcoming 2016)
Altar of the Wilderness (forthcoming 2016)

Books on audio

Narrated by James Drury, "The Virginian"
Published by Books in Motion (www.booksinmotion.com)
Available through the author at www.kirbyjonas.com

The Dansing Star
Death of an Eagle
Legend of the Tumbleweed
Lady Winchester

Yaqui Gold, narrated by Gene Engene
The Secret of Two Hawks, narrated by Kevin Foley (Winner, 2010 Spur Award from Western Writers of America, "Best Western Audiobook")
Knight of the Ribbons, narrated by Rusty Nelson
Drygulch to Destiny, narrated by Kirby Jonas

To order books, go to www.kirbyjonas.com or write to:

Howling Wolf Publishing
1611 City Creek Road
Pocatello ID 83204

Or send email to: kirby@kirbyjonas.com